LOVE THREE WAYS

By Jean Kirby

 New Generation Publishing

Also by Jean Kirby

Cancer The Heartache The Truth

Three Ways to Die

A Key, A Garden, A Cottage A mystery lies within

IF ONLY

He was a loving husband of many years but then things changed.

He was so calm but then something happened inside him. Something snapped and he became a different person. Or did he?

UNFORGIVING

You fall in love, you think you know them, then you realise the mistake.

Only then, do you do something you will regret the rest of your life?

FORBIDDEN LOVE

Sometimes because of the work you do, love cannot be pursued.

Then it is re-awakened with terrifying consequences.

IF ONLY

Chapter 1

He sat in the darkened room with his head in his hands, wondering how he would cope with the situation. His wife had become this monster that was spinning out of control. He had to stop this madness somehow.

Looking back, they had been happily married, and had children they had both wanted, but when they left home there was this void they both felt. It was more than that though. She became over time this person he did not recognise as the woman he married all those years ago.

It was soon after Susan, their daughter, went off to University and David, their son, found a job down in London. That is when the cracks started to appear in the marriage.

At first, it was small things, not really noticeable, a few comments here and there as he remembered looking back, about his driving at first. That was bound to happen, he thought, as they shared the car. He could not afford to run two when he retired so they had to share it. He had to drive her to her part-time job, so he could have the car. While he was driving she would complain he was not going the right way or not the quickest way or he was in the wrong lane. It became so that it grated on him so much and for a quiet life he let her drive the car to work instead of him. When that happened she still told him how good a driver she was and he was useless at driving. He just sat calmly as he always did and agreed with her for a quiet life.

This is how it started, the drip, drip like Chinese torture, but he was a patient and quite man and did not like fuss in any way. After the criticism of his driving she moved onto other things, his washing up of the dishes, plates had smears on them. He had stored them wrong in the cupboards, ever though she had used the same place for years, it was wrong! In the end to appease her he stopped doing the washing up. That upset her and so she complained he was lazy for not helping, he could not win whatever he did for her. She was hard to please. Her mood swings he could not anticipate anymore, it was like she was becoming this stranger.

The other thing that happened over the months which really upset him was the love making they had both enjoyed for a lot of years. She would not make love to him anymore which started with excuses, so much so he gave up making advances in bed. That hurt him dearly as he still loved her and she would not even allow cuddles or kisses, as she would pull away. It was like walking on egg shells in the bedroom.

He had mentioned to her several times that maybe she should seek help from the doctor but she would not speak to him for several days after he suggested it. He had looked on the internet to see what the problem was and it all pointed to the menopause which the doctors could help with various medications, but she would not listen to him.

He was talking to his mate, Charles, one day and mentioned his wife's moods and he told him, "Lucy went through the menopause and she would cry at anything. It was also the moods she was having which was not her. We talked about it and went off to the doctors together, to get help."

Grant said, "That is okay if the wife talks to you in a normal way, but I cannot get through to Doris."

Charles shrugged, "What about your daughter, can't she speak to her?"

Grant replied, "We don't see much of her, especially since she went off to University and has a job there as well. Anyway they were never close."

Charles commiserated with him, drank his beer, they then both stood up to go out of the pub, their local. It was great sometimes, living in a village, to be able to walk to the pub and not have to watch what you drink, as you were walking home not driving.

They both left the pub wishing each other a good night. They both turned in opposite directions to go home. Grant was calm in himself as he always was and thought to himself that Charles was lucky that his wife was so considerate about things. He arrived back at his house and put the key in the door and turning the key, wondered what was waiting for him from his wife, or whether she would still be up waiting for him, to give him the ear bashing he always received and expected.

As he opened the door no light was on downstairs, just the landing one. She must have gone to bed, which made him more worried at what she had left him downstairs. It was affecting his nerves and made it more painful to be in her company, but he would not walk away from the marriage as it was not the right thing to do. He was at breaking point and possibly he was heading for a nervous breakdown.

He shut the door behind him, making sure he locked it correctly. It had got to the stage where he was questioning himself in the way he did things, was he going mad? He hung his coat up and then saw the sign she had left him. It was instructing him to make sure he hung his coat correctly and his shoes were left in a certain way as not to leave dirt on the carpet. He could not take this any more in silence, then a sudden rage overtook him which had built up inside for so long, he just snapped. Mind blank – he could see through his eyes but had no control, it was not him, it was another person, storming in the kitchen picking up the knife from the rack. This was not him. He was shouting inside – stop, stop! But he had no control, but he loved her!

This other person was striding up the stairs towards their bedroom – you are a calm, kind person, stop – but all he could do was watch his body he had no control over. This other person inside him walked up to the bed where his wife lay asleep, the sheets moving with her every breath, as she only had a sheet over her. He remembered she was always hot, because of the hot flushes she had. Then he saw the hand with the knife come down, with the knife going into her body, so many times, he could not recall. He had to close his mind to what was happening. Was he dreaming? He opened his eyes to a scene he could not comprehend, blood was everywhere. He looked down at his hand holding the knife covered in blood. That was when reality hit him and he collapsed on the floor.

He started crying hysterically, "What have I done?"

He started to hyper- ventilate, he needed help. He dragged himself to the phone in the bedroom and dialled 999. Someone answered. He struggled to talk and get the words out of his mouth, "Help, I need help, I can't breath and I think," he paused looking down at his hands, "I am injured."

The operator kept him talking, trying to get information out of him but he was in shock and had breathing difficulty. He had to drag himself to the door to let them in, but his legs would not allow him to stand, so using his bloody hands he dragged himself towards the door along the hallway. He did not know how but he managed it, stretched and pulled himself up the door to open the door with the key. He fell back exhausted and still breathless, lost consciousness, as the sound of sirens were playing in his head, then blackness, he passed out.

Chapter 2

The police and ambulance arrived at the bungalow. The police tried the door and slowly opened it but Grant's body was stopping it being opened fully. It was opened enough for the officer to squeeze through followed by the paramedic. The police officer stooped down first towards the body, noticing the bloody hand first then the blood splattered clothing, and he pointed to the paramedic to check the body to make sure he was not the victim. He nodded and then the officer started to search the premises, not knowing what he would find.

He followed the trail of blood which led him to the bedroom, where he saw the blood soaked body in the bedroom. There was too much blood on the bed and sheets, for the victim to have survived and he did not want to contaminate the scene so called for back up and hopefully forensics would be able to decide what went on. After calling it in he went back to the body by the door and the paramedic who was assessing him.

The officer asked, "Is he breathing and are there any wounds on him?"

The paramedic replied, "No sign of wounds anywhere so not sure whose blood it is on him."

The officer replied, "I think the unlucky person in the bedroom in the bed is my guess."

The paramedic turned back to the body as the officer inquired whether the man could be moved, and the paramedic said, "We need to get him to hospital so we can do some tests, as he is still unconscious."

They gently moved him so that the door could be

opened to put him on the stretcher from the ambulance and transfer him to hospital. An officer was appointed to go in the ambulance to hospital in case he regained consciousness and could tell them what had happened.

They were in the process of transferring the man to the ambulance when Detective Clark arrived, along with other officers and the forensics team.

Clark got out of his car and went over to the officer at the back of the ambulance. He updated the detective, then turned to instruct the head of the forensic team, Rix, and asked for a bag to put the man's clothes into once he was in hospital, due to the clothes holding evidence from the scene of the crime. The officer who was inside the ambulance with the man, was handed the bag and instructed what to do and was given gloves as well. The doors of the ambulance were then shut and they went off with the lights flashing and the sirens on.

Clark turned and headed for the property with the forensic team. He put covers on his feet and gloves on his hands and followed the team. Clark did not want to upset Rix as he had had several confrontations with him over the years for not taking precautions not to contaminate the scene of the crime.

The officer at the door pointed them towards the bedroom. Photographs were being taken, and the weapon on the floor had been marked with a number. Rix approached the body and nodded to the photographer that it was okay. He pulled the sheet gently off the body and noticed it was a woman lying there on the bed. The blood had soaked through the sheet, her nightie and a large area around where the body lay. He could see puncture marks, many of them made through the nightie.

Rix turned to Clark, "I think we can agree at what we see, she was murdered with the knife that is on the floor. We will take swabs to make sure the blood is the victim's and not the man taken to hospital."

He went on to say, "No struggle is evident so we presume she was asleep when the attack happened. Can't say anymore, but need to speak to the man, who we presume was the husband, or was he an intruder?"

Clark said, "Well there was no sign of forced entry, in fact the 999 call was from the man taken to hospital, who had no injuries despite the amount of blood found on him, mainly the hands and torso."

Rix instructed one of his men to go down to the hospital to gain more samples than just clothes the man was wearing. Turning to Clark, he said, "Is that alright with you detective?"

"Yes he can liaise with the officer down at the hospital," Clark said.

Clark turned as his eyes scanned over the bedroom wondering, why would a husband kill his wife in such a frenzy, and in cold blood? He turned his attention to other rooms. He walked into the lounge and saw photographs of them both together, with what he presumed was the son and daughter. He then stood for a moment and looked around the room. The rooms seemed too tidy. Like it was not lived in, not a homely house you would expect perhaps? He felt there was something wrong, gut feeling again, but he could not put his finger on it.

He came out of the room into the hall and noticed by the coat stand a notice stuck to the wall. It was an order of what the husband had to do. Strange. Then he found several others in the kitchen, inside and outside the cupboards, next to the kettle and toaster.

Clark thought, what would happen to the husband

if the wife found he had not done these orders. Maybe this was not as straight forward a case as he thought. He decided he needed more background information on this couple. He called an officer over to him at the door and ordered a house to house to gain information about the couple, their movements and did anyone notice anything different between them. Hopefully he thought a little more help would come from the husband taken to hospital, when he regained consciousness. Clark needed to build a picture up of the life in the house of the Dales. Yes he had found letters addressed to them, so at least he knew their surname.

He had opened the letters and discovered it was Doris and Grant. They needed to search for contact details of the son and daughter, to contact them. He would get uniform onto that. He took a picture from the photo frame which he thought it would help them in the investigation.

Rix came to Clark to say they had finished and that the body could now be moved and he would do the post-mortem as soon as he could and report back. He told Clark he would organise the removal if that was okay.

Clark half laughed, "Typical Rix, are you sure you don't want to swop jobs?"

Rix gave a rude reply, which Clark was used to but took it in his stride as they had known each other for some time and they socialised in the local for a beer many times. Rix had helped Clark solve many cases and was an immense help to him, an asset he did not want to lose.

Clark continued looking in the lounge for a contact list, address book, anything with the son or daughter's contact details. He found an old address book which looked like it had been used for many years. He flicked through it and found what he was looking for and then left the property.

The property was left cordoned off with his officers on site and some doing the house knocking for information about the couple. He was hoping that they would gain more information to enable him to get a better picture about the relationship of Doris and Grant.

Then he got into his car and headed towards St David's hospital, hoping that Grant had regained consciousness and he could throw some light on what had happened at the property. Clark drove, it was still dark and he thought to himself, it will be a long day with everything to do now. He was glad he had no wife and children like some officers as with this job it was hard on relationships and some of the officer's struggled.

He arrived at St David's hospital and went into A&E, spoke to someone at reception and was directed to the doctor's station. He arrived and came across three doctors in full discussion about a patient when he said, "Excuse me but I am looking for Grant Dale who was brought in from a crime scene I am investigating." They all turned at once towards him, then one of them spoke, "Yes an interesting gentleman, I will take you to him. He is very confused at the moment and cannot remember why he is here. It looks like he may have short term amnesia caused by shock."

The detective told the doctor as they walked what they knew so far and was now concerned that Grant could not remember, he thought how convenient it was for him. They walked into the cubicle, the doctor leading the way and Clark following. The officer sitting next to Grant stood up when seeing Clark. Then Clark looked at Grant. His look was semi-vacant as if searching Clark's face for recognition. Clark addressed him.

"I am Detective Clark and you are I believe Grant Dale. Is this correct?"

Grant shrugged his shoulders and said, "If that is my name. I am a little fuzzy on remembering things. All I can remember is waking up in the ambulance and being asked questions about who I am. It's very confusing at the moment for me. They also took off all my clothes and put them in a bag and did something with my hands and fingernails before I was allowed to wash my hands. I am not sure why I had blood on them and the doctors have said it was not my blood as they have found no wounds. Can you help clear a few things up for me Detective?"

Clark cleared his throat. "We believe you are Grant Dale who lives at 48 Willow Tree Lane and that you are married to Doris and have a son and daughter. Can I show you a picture to see if that jogs your memory?"

Grant said, "Yes", as Clark took the picture he took from the house, out of his pocket and passed it to Grant. Grant took a long hard look at the picture and then looked up at the Detective. He said, "I think I know them but their names evade me," then handed the picture back to Clark.

The Detective went on, "Can you remember what you were doing last night at all?"

Grant scratched his head, "Probably went to the pub as usual, I am not quite sure. Is it important?"

Clark went on to ask Grant could he remember anything that would help them about last night. Was there a break in or were he and his wife the only people in the house? Clark thought he was going to have to tell him to see what reaction he would get as Grant seemed unable to give him the information he wanted at this time.

Clark said, "Mr Dale I am sorry to say that when we came to your property after you phoned 999, we found yourself unconscious and a body in the bedroom which we believe is your wife Doris. Do you understand what I am saying Mr Dale?"

Grant looked up at Clark's face and asked him to repeat the question and then Grant said, "Are you saying someone has killed my wife?" The Detective nodded. That was when Grant reacted.

"No you must be mistaken she can't be dead, I love her, and what will I do?" Grant's expression then changed and tears started falling down his cheeks, as he repeated that she can't be dead and who would do such a thing. Then the sobbing and tears just flowed and he became hysterical. Clark had to call a nurse to calm him down. Once the nurse had come and calmed Grant down, Clark said that an officer would stay at his bedside until he could start recalling things that happened last night.

Clark turned to go when Grant said, "What about the children?"

Clark replied that he would be in touch with them as soon as possible and let them know where he was. He turned and left, wondering whether what he had seen was an act by a very devious person, or a genuine one. Time would tell.

Clark was given the forensics bag as he left and walked out of the hospital, putting the bag into his boot of his car. He got in and drove off, thinking this is going to be a difficult case to prove if Grant does not get his memory back.

Chapter 3

Clark arrived at the police station. It was a modern building by today's standards, and had the forensics department under the same roof, which made life easier for everyone. He headed for their office and hoped that Rix was there. He pushed the door open, yes, he was at his desk. Clark thought to himself, this guy never sleeps! But like himself, he was married to the job, except Rix was younger than him, but time doing this job, would eventually tell on him.

Rix looked up and saw the bag containing Grant's clothes covered in blood, along with smaller sample bags which would hopefully confirm it was the victim's blood. In the smaller sample bags were swabs taken from Grant's hands and under his fingernails just in case they helped confirming things. Rix's philosophy was you can never have too much evidence.

Clark put the bag on his desk and Rix thanked him and said, "Has this guy confessed to the murder then?"

Clark's eyebrows moved up and down, it was his way many noticed over the years. He replied, "No, it's complicated."

Rix looked puzzled and asked, "How?"

Clark explained about Grant not remembering what happened and his reaction to the news about his wife's death. Rix let out a sigh. "You have a problem on your hands then. Is it real amnesia or his he faking it? Glad it is you who has to deal with that side of it."

Clark laughed, "Thanks."

He turned and walked out heading for his office where he would start to formalise the way forward with this case. He needed to speak to someone in the medical profession and get some reports done on Grant's amnesia problem. Then he would have to wait for the autopsy report and the forensic evidence which will take some time. He needed to be careful everything was done right, otherwise he might not get the right result he was after, in his mind, at the moment.

He entered his central office and it was a hive of activity. Some of the officers came up to him and updated him on what they had so far. Clark gave one of them the task of contacting the children, giving him the contact details he had found at the property and hoping they were up to date. He wanted them to come to the police station first so he could give them the news before going to see their father. He made it clear to the officer that instruction was to be followed to the letter.

He also needed background information on the family and the life they had, which would help maybe to see if Grant's amnesia was real or pretend. He needed to tread carefully. He left them to carry on, while he went into his office, after he had got himself a coffee. He sat down at his desk and reflected on the cases he had come across in his time: mainly murder cases, but with the experience of other cases as well this was going to be just that little bit different for him, he thought. He needed Grant to talk and he needed information on what sort of person he was, so he could piece a picture together.

He swallowed the last of his coffee, and walked into the outer office. They had the board up which helped them put information on: the victim, not pretty pictures of her from the scene of the crime, and the murder weapon picture at the scene. The knife had been confirmed that it was from the kitchen, after a search, from a set which had one missing. There was also a picture of the family (taken from the property) including the son and daughter in it, pictures of the blood stained clothing taken from Grant, courtesy of Rix. He was always helpful as he knew how Clark worked.

The board looked a little empty, but hopefully as information came in it would soon be full. Clark got every body's attention. He needed to inform them about Grant in hospital and whether he had lost his memory genuinely or was putting it on. This could be temporary due to the shock, but he needed two volunteers to do shifts at the hospital between themselves, he was not bothered how they sorted it. One of them had to be at Grant's side all the time just in case he started to remember things, anything however small.

Two of the officers spoke out to say they would do it, so Clark gave them the hospital details and they left. He turned and addressed the rest of them. "It is a small village, someone must know Grant, socialised with him in some way. We want to put together a picture of this man, his hobbies, his movements, whether he was a good guy or a bad one, we need to know. Once we have interviewed the children, we will put a request for any information about the family or anyone who knew them outside the village. Now go and do your jobs."

From the hush of the room there grew the noise of everyone agreeing and then officers leaving, some still staying, making phone calls, a hive of industry. Let's hope we get somewhere, Clark thought.

Clark returned to his office and started looking at the evidence so far - not a lot - when the telephone rang. It was Rix. He confirmed the blood on the clothing of Grant's was in fact of the deceased, his wife. He also confirmed the same with the samples taken from under Grant's fingernails and hands. They all matched therefore the conclusion at this time was Grant used the knife on his wife, and no one else was indicated. Rix said that the post-mortem would be done tomorrow, the report would be a few days after, that was if no drugs were found. Otherwise it would take longer.

Clark thanked Rix and said, "It is high time you and I had a drink again, together, last time was good."

Rix laughed, "We sound like we have nothing else to do, I will keep that in mind for the near future."

Clark put the telephone down as a knock came at the door, which opened. An officer informed him Grant's son would be in the office first thing and said he understood that he was not to visit his father first, until he was made aware of the situation. The daughter was more difficult and wanted to see her father first but was told she would be turned away from the hospital by an officer and really she needed to come in for the full story before she visited her father. This was a murder enquiry and she needed to do as instructed. She calmed down a little and said she would be arriving in the morning but was not sure what time. She was thanked for her co-operation in the matter.

Clark thanked him and said it was a good idea for them both to be escorted to hospital together, as he could foresee problems ahead. Clark looked up at the clock and said to the officer he would be off shortly as it had been a long night.

Clark thought a good night sleep and he would be ready to interview the son and daughter in the morning. Fatigue had started catching up with him and no amount of coffee would keep him awake.

He stood up to leave, and as he shut the door to his office and walking through the main office, turned to the officer and said, "Anything of importance comes up ring me."

"Yes, sir," The officer replied.

Clark was really tired now. He drove home with loud music playing to keep him alert. He pulled up his drive and went inside his house. He went straight upstairs, into his bedroom, pulled his clothes off and fell on the bed exhausted.

Chapter 4

The alarm woke Clark at 7am. He showered and shaved, and he felt good. He grabbed a banana and some strawberries, chopped them up and added them to the milk in the machine. It whizzed for a while. When it stopped he took it and drank, that was good. He then drove to the office and arrived just after 8am and parked up.

He entered the main office and saw fresh faces, and they wanted updating on the case. One of the officers approached him after he had talked to the new ones on the case.

He said, "The son of Mr Dale will be here at 10am. He is coming up from London on the train. His daughter will be in at 11am. She will be driving up from University which she attends. I did not catch exactly which one but will leave that detail to you Sir, when you interview her." Clark nodded and thanked the officer.

Clark addressed the room, "Do we have any information from the neighbours or people living in the village yet?" he asked.

One officer, Jenkins, who had been into the shop, post office and then the public house, had been given a name of a friend of Grant's.

So Jenkins said, "Yes, Grant was a regular drinker in the public house and was always with this friend the landlord had said."

Clark asked, "Do we know where this guy lives and has anyone been to see him yet?"

Jenkins replied, "We have a vague address but are checking the electoral register for a more accurate one. Once we have it, how do you want me to play it with him, informal in the home or invite him to come into the station?"

Clark thought for a while then said, "Keep it simple. There has been an incident at the Dales house and you believe he knew Grant and would he come along to the station to help with enquiries. See what his reaction is and then decide whether to do a quick interview in the home or if he offers to come in himself. I will leave you to judge the situation." The officer nodded.

Clark then turned to Joe Reynolds, one of his officers who had worked with him on many cases in the past. "Joe, I want you in on the interviews with me." Joe nodded to acknowledge him.

They both walked off towards the interview rooms they were going to use, Clark turned towards Joe and said, "Hopefully we are going to learn what sort of person we are dealing with once we have spoken to the son and daughter."

Clark opened one of the doors to the interview rooms, dropped his paperwork onto the desk and Joe did the same along with a note pad. Joe went off to get Grant's son, when he arrived, which he hoped was shortly.

Clark sat down and opened the file, and looked at what they had so far, which was not a lot. He looked up when the door opened and Joe walked Grant's son into the room and introduced him as David to Clark, who went on to say that this was an informal meeting just to share information they both had. They all sat down. Clark started to explain the situation that had brought them to now.

Clark started to tell David that they were called to his father's property via a 999 call and needed David just to confirm it was the correct address. Clark asked, "David can you confirm that this is your parents' address."

"Yes," David replied.

Clark went on, "Can you also confirm these are your parents, Grant and Doris Dale?" and he showed him the picture that he had taken from the property. David nodded.

Clark went on, "I believe therefore, the lady we found dead at the property was your mother, but we need to have a formal identification from yourself to be certain. If you want to wait for your sister, I understand but we do need to speak to her first before you can talk to her under the circumstances which I will explain shortly, why."

He could see David digesting everything that had been said so far before he said, "Is Dad okay? Why could he not do it?"

Clark cleared his throat before speaking, "Your father is okay, is detained in hospital and is under observation due his loss of memory. We hope this will be temporary which may have been caused by the shock of seeing your mother lying dead, we think. As he and your mother seem to be the only."

"Hang on a minute," David said, not letting Clark finish his sentence, "Are you saying my father killed my mother, well that is preposterous he would not hurt a fly." He folded his arms across his chest in a defensive way.

Clark went on to explain that evidence found at the scene was pointing to his father committing the crime. He went on to say they had not fully interviewed his father due to doctor's advice at this time. They said he needed to be properly assessed about his mental state and the doctors were organising the correct department to deal with it. Therefore if he,

22

David went to see his father, he must not mention anything about the situation at this stage. The doctors said too much information may not help and he could completely switch off. David nodded as if he understood the situation, but at the same time not believing what had been said about his mother.

Clark then asked, just for the record where David was the night in question at approximately 11pm. David nodded, understanding and stated that he was out with friends from work and he could get their contact details if necessary. Clark thanked him and asked if he wanted a cup of tea or coffee while he waited, until Clark saw his sister in a separate room. David replied, "Coffee please with milk and a spoonful of sugar, thanks."

Clark stood up and opened the door, turned, and David stood and shook his hand and thanked him. Clark said an officer would bring him his coffee shortly and he would bring his sister in once he had spoken to her. He nodded.

Clark and Joe left the room and went along the corridor to another interview room and put their papers down again. Joe said he would check to see if the daughter had arrived yet. It was not long afterwards that he appeared at the door with the daughter. She entered, Clark rising up from his seat and shook her hand, introducing himself to her. He invited her to sit and Joe joined Clark on his side of the desk.

Clark said he needed a few things confirmed first, a formality. Was she Susan Dale daughter of Grant and Doris Dale? She nodded. Clark noticed she was very controlled in her body language. Then confirmed her address. Again she nodded. He went on to say that a body was found at her parent's house and that they believe it was in fact her mother Doris and they needed a formal identification from someone in the family. She nodded saying yes at the same time.

She showed no emotion on her face, just a normal expression. Strange thought Clark, mother and daughter relationship should be closer?

She then said, "What about Dad, can he not identify her, or was he injured?"

Clark cleared his throat before he spoke and said, "Well actually we believe on the evidence we found at the scene from both on your father and mother it seems your father may have been responsible for her death. But due to your father losing his memory and not knowing what happened, he is in hospital under the care of doctors who believe that due to the trauma of what happened it had put his brain into shock, so he has no memory of it.

Susan muttered, "She pushed him so hard."

Clark said, "What did you say?" She said, "Nothing."

Clark went on, "We know this is a shock and any help about your parent's relationship would help us piece together the picture of how this happened."

Susan showed no emotion except for the hands screwing up into a fist. Was she hiding something, then she said, "Well you might as well know there was no love lost between mum and me. Especially when I went off to University, it was a relief to be out of the house, away from her."

Clark pushed, "Why?"

Susan relaxed her hands a little and spoke, "It was small things I noticed at first. Dad was laid back, a gentle giant. He put up with her ordering him, little things at first. Then it developed over the months and years that Dad could not do anything right no matter how he did it. I pulled her up the last time I was home, just overnight, but she snapped my head off and said it was none of my business. I left the next day. It started a few years ago when she started going through the menopause. It changed her to this angry uncaring person. I tried to suggest she get help from the GP but she just ignored me and would not discuss it. I was wondering if Dad had finally snapped and could not cope any more. Like I said he was a gentle giant and would do anything to please her."

Clark asked, "So your Dad did not have a temper or short fuse? He would not be aggressive towards your Mum in any way, even with her ordering him around?"

"I am not sure, he was a very easy going, and I can imagine the last two years have been hard for him," she replied.

Clark final said, "That has been very helpful and for the record where were you on the night in question at 11pm?"

She smiled and replied, "Actually in bed with my boyfriend, we share a house. I can give you his details if you want them?"

Clark said, "That's fine, we just needed to ask, just routine."

She nodded. Clark stood and said he would take her to see her brother now in the other room waiting for her. They left the room, went along the corridor and he opened another door. David rose and rushed to meet her.

Clark told them to take their time and have as long as they needed together to talk things over. He said an officer would stay outside the door and for them to let this officer know as and when they were ready, to identify their mother. They both nodded and thanked him. Clark left Joe outside the room to escort them to a room in the forensics area where Mrs Dale's body was.

Clark returned to the main office when an officer approached him and said, "Can I have a word? I have some news on Grants friend he drinks with." He followed Clark into his office, then Clark turned towards him and said, "Talk, what have you got?"

He repeated what he was told. "Grant did have a drinking buddy, Charles. Charles and his wife Lucy are friends also with both of them, in fact for some years. In fact they had a lot to say, too much so had to stop them before I asked if one or both would come to the station so we could put the information on record. They agreed and are coming in this afternoon."

Clark thought a picture was emerging of Grant, but what about the abnormality of his mental functioning state. How was he able to exercise willpower or control physical acts in accordance with rational judgement? It just did not add up, and now Grant had amnesia of the event. He needed the doctors to tell him what was wrong with him or was he just faking it all?

Clark was looking forward to talking with Charles, Grant's drinking pal and friend to give him more insight into the character of Grant. He thanked his officer, who left then Clark grabbed a coffee and ate his banana, thinking. Just as he had finished, Joe popped his head round his office door to say, "Both the son and daughter have confirmed the deceased was in fact Doris their mother. They are now going to the hospital to see their father and understand they have to be careful when they talk to him, and be guided by the doctors due to his state of mind." Clark thanked him and updated Joe on the information about Charles, Grant's friend. He told Joe to grab something to eat before he joined him in the interview. Joe nodded and left.

Clark's telephone rang. They said that Charles, Grant's friend had arrived, and Clark said he would send someone down to fetch him up to the interview rooms. He put the telephone down and called Joe. He came to his door with a half-eaten sandwich in his hand, and Clark asked him to go and bring Charles up to the interview rooms, when he had finished his sandwich.

Joe asked him, "Which room do you want me to bring him to boss?"

Clark said, "Interview room 3 should be okay."

Joe acknowledged and went off to finish his sandwich. Clark picked up his pad and pen and the file with information so far gathered, and went off to the room to wait for Joe and this guy Charles.

In a short while, Joe opened the door and showed Charles in, Clark stood and shook his hand and offered him a seat. Joe and Clark sat opposite him.

Clark started, "I believe you can help us with our enquiries about the Dale family and you are prepared to make a statement, is that correct?"

Charles nodded but looks nervous. Clark reassures him that the interview would be recorded, typed up and he would be allowed to alter if necessary anything he had said before signing it. Charles relaxed a little.

Clark started the recorder, and said, "Please state your name, address for the records, please."

Charles did so. Clark then asked, "How do you know Grant and Doris Dale, please in your own words, we can stop at any time."

Charles nodded, shuffled a little closer to the desk

and started his story.

Charles and his wife, Lucy had moved into the village five years ago and had bumped into the Dales one day at the village fete. They got friendly and would go out together as two couples until two years ago. Lucy was finding it more difficult to be friends with Doris, so they stopped going out as couples but Charles still went out with Grant. They met at the pub regularly, especially when they both stopped working. Then Doris started restricting when Grant could go out to the pub.

Clark interrupted and asked, "What do you mean, surely he could go whenever he wanted to?"

Charles replied, "No, she made life so difficult for him in so many ways that Grant wanted a quiet life, so towed the line with her. He was like that. He would want to keep the peace, so did as he was told. I think I would have had a blazing row with my wife if she treated me like that."

"Go on," Clark said.

Charles said, "One day Grant asked me if my wife had changed due to her age being the same. I told him about our experience when Lucy went through the change, where we both went to see the doctor, together, to get her help. She got the help she needed and we went back on an even keel. Grant tried the same with Doris and was rebuffed by her and given the silent treatment for even suggesting her going to see her doctor."

Charles went on to say that Grant's life was made hell, his wife Doris would leave instructions around the house for him to do this and that. If he did not do things she made him suffer by not cooking, washing or ironing for him, she could be hurtful. Grant was so calm through all of this, he was unbelievable what he put up with.

Clark then asked, "The last night you went out with him, tell me about that."

"Yes," Charles said. "It was our usual night for going drinking at the pub in the village, handy to walk to. We had our usual three pints, put the world to rights, but he never said anything new about their relationship, it was the same for all I knew."

Clark asked, "Nothing different? And you saw him leave?"

"Yes, we went out together. He went one way and I the other," Charles replied.

Clark said, "That was the last time you saw Grant?"

Charles replied, "Yes, and can you tell me that he is okay, alive, as no one will give me a straight answer?"

Clark cleared his throat and said, "I am sorry to say that a body which was found at their property, has now been identified as Doris. We believe on the evidence found so far that Grant may have killed her, but," Clark holding his hand up to stop Charles from talking went on to say, "Grant is in hospital, unhurt and is under medical supervision due to memory loss."

Charles stuttered, "No, poor man, how can that be, he would not hurt anyone."

Clark recalled someone else remarking about this, about Grant. He went on to say only family are allowed to see him at this time and that the son and daughter were with him.

Charles nodded and enquired when he needed to sign his statement. Clark looked at Joe, then Joe said tomorrow but they would contact him to come in, as and when it was ready.

They all stood up, Clark shook Charles hand and thanked him for the information and Joe showed him out. Clark took the tape out of the machine, left the interview room and closed the door behind him.

Chapter 5

The next day Clark went to the hospital to check on the progress of Grant's health and to ask the doctors if he was able to be questioned without affecting his mental state.

Clark arrived at the hospital and spoke to the staff and doctors who were looking after Grant. They ushered him into their office to talk. The doctors wanted Clark to understand that they had diagnosed Grant with dissociative amnesia. Grant could remember going to the pub and coming home, opening the door and going to hang his coat up and then nothing except waking up in the ambulance and being disorientated. He was a little better now he had seen his son and daughter. They were under strict orders not to talk about the event. Grant had been asking the doctors more details about his wife's death but they had avoided telling him the truth as they were not sure of his reactions and it could make matters worse.

The doctors went on to say, "Dissociative amnesia has various frameworks about how and why dissociative amnesia might occur. Many believe that it occurs because the person has experienced adverse emotional consequences of trauma or by repressing the experience from conscious awareness. We believe a proper psychiatric report on this person is required to evaluate his mental state."

Clark asked, "Can I interview him at the station?"

The doctor replied, "Yes if a doctor and solicitor is present to assure that Grant is not pressured in any way."

Clark asked to go and see Grant. They both stood

up and left the room together heading for Grant's bed. He was dressed and stood up when Clark entered the room.

Grant asked, "Can you tell me what is happening as no one will tell me?"

Clark introduced himself and said that he needed to come to the police station to help answer some questions about what happened to his wife.

Grant then said, "I have a vague memory of someone saying she is dead, which I could not believe, as she had a strong heart, but people said they would not go into detail how she died and I had to wait for you to explain things to me. I will go to the station with you and my son said he has arranged for a solicitor to be present as well, why I cannot understand."

Clark asked the officer, who had been with Grant, to take him down to the car when he was ready and that he would follow shortly himself. Clark left the room and found the doctor to ask who was coming to the station. He was too busy but had been in touch with a GP they used to oversee cases at the police station and had filled him in with the details so he could be on hand if Grant lost it again. Clark agreed that would be acceptable.

Clark also asked the doctor to email the report, if any, on what they had talked about, the condition itself and the psychiatric report as and when it was ready. Clark left the doctor and headed for the car. Grant was already inside the car with the officer. Clark got in and drove off in silence to the station. Clark was going over in his mind how he was going to handle this interview, slowly and precisely, as he was not sure whether Grant was putting on an act or had truly lost his memory of what happened that night.

They arrived and asked the officer to take Grant through to interview room two and he would shortly follow. On entering the station Clark was surprised to see waiting for Grant, his son and a gentleman next to him, his solicitor he presumed. They both stood as they came in, Grant acknowledging his son and then David said, "This is Mr Jackson, Dad's solicitor," to Clark.

Clark said, "That is fine, can you follow the officer accompanying your client please but David you will have to wait out here please." David nodded, understanding the situation and the possible seriousness of the case.

Clark followed them into the interview room and asked the police officer to go and find Joe to come and join them for the interview. Clark shut the door behind the officer as they all took their seats. Water was available on the table for everyone and Grant poured himself a glass.

The door opened and Joe entered with the files, note pad and tape, which he handed Clark, and he put the tape into the machine. Clark went over what would happen next and asked was Grant in agreement. He said he was. Clark said he could stop at any time and there was a GP available if he felt unwell. Grant nodded.

They started with Clark clearing his throat, "Can you state for the tape your full name and address please," he asked. Grant did so.

Clark then asked, "Can you tell us in your own words what happened on the evening of the 10th May, from say 5pm that evening."

Grant gathered his thoughts as best he could and said, "I had my tea about six that evening. Doris never does my tea on the night I go out for a drink with Charles, she thinks I should not go out for a drink." He went on, "I met Charles as usual at 7.30pm in the local pub, The Royal Oak it's called. We sat and talked about sports and new topics, and had three pints of beer as always. We finished up and left about eleven. I opened the door, we both walked out, Charles turned to go home, and I went in the other direction. I walked towards the house and put the key in the door. The lock is a little stiff. Went in and walked straight to the coat stand to hang my coat up and take my shoes off. Then noticed Doris had put up a notice, her usual orders to make sure I did everything correctly and then nothing. I can't remember anything until in the ambulance and hospital."

Clark said, "So you cannot remember what you did to your wife?"

Grant looked puzzled, "What do you mean, how do you know what I did to my wife?"

Clark stated, for the tape and everyone that was present, "I believe from the evidence found at your property and from your clothes we removed from you at the hospital, that you stabbed your wife multiple times until she was dead."

Grant went as white as a sheet, took a sip of water while looking blank faced and turned to the solicitor next to him. He regained his composure and asked, "How could I have done such a thing? I loved her."

Clark went on to say, "Maybe after all these years of being dictated to you just snapped, not knowing what you were doing until it was too late? Then panicked finding yourself covered in her blood you rang 999 for help?"

Grant said, "I rang 999, when?"

Clark replied, "Looks like it was after you realised what you had done. Blood was found on your clothes, which was your wife's, as well as your hands, telephone and door handle, then you unlocked the door before passing out."

Mr Jackson, Grant's solicitor asked, "Can I have access to the forensic results? I would also ask my client to have a doctor's assessment for his state of mind, which I understand was done when my client was taken into hospital."

Clark replied, "Yes, we have evidence that will confirm that Mr Grant Dale stabbed his wife. We also have the reports from the hospital, verbal, but have requested it in writing that Mr Dale maybe suffering from dissociative amnesia which is a state due to strong emotional stress, the realisation of what he had done."

Clark went on, "We therefore have to charge Mr Grant Dale with the murder of his wife. He will remain in custody until he is brought before the court to be formally charged and for him to agree to the plea or whatever you decide for your client."

Clark turned to Grant and said, "Do you have anything to say?"

Grant looked at his solicitor, then back at Clark and said, "I am telling you I can't remember," in a raised and agitated voice.

Clark rang for the GP to be brought in to calm Grant down. He stopped the tape. The door opened and the GP came in so Clark said, "I will leave you for a moment and let the GP check you. Mr Dale, please calm down, I know this is hard but please co-operate."

Grant nodded as he sat down and the GP approached him to check him. Clark left the room with Joe and stood outside the room. Joe asked, "What happens to Grant?"

Clark thought for a while, "He will be remanded in custody, maybe not prison because of his mental state, maybe hospital? That is up to the solicitor. There will be psychiatric reports about whether he does not remember what he did or whether he is faking it, that is for doctors to prove. The CPS will look at the evidence and agree whether to prosecute. We have to collect all the evidence we have and take it to court. Whether the evidence of being a brow beaten man who has a placid demeanour will help him, it will be up to the courts to decide. They could argue he had an abnormality of mental functioning, meaning a state of mind so different from that of an ordinary human being, that the reasonable person would term it abnormal behaviour. It covers the ability to exercise will power or to control physical acts in accordance with rational judgement. In other words, did he know what he was doing or not. It will be the jury who have to decide on the evidence put before them."

Clark hoped that with all the evidence they had that the jury would do the right thing, but in this case what was the right thing?

Joe looked at him puzzled, "Surely guilty of course, don't you think?"

Clark half smiled and said, "The jury, Joe, the jury."

Chapter 6

It took six months before the case of Grant Dale came to court. Clark was called to give evidence. Grant's solicitor had many psychiatric reports stating that Grant had suffered dissociative amnesia which he might never recover from. They said that they believed that dissociative amnesia occurs because the person experienced adverse emotional consequences of trauma or by repressing the experience from conscious awareness.

The plea was Voluntary Manslaughter with diminished responsibilities; meaning in a state of mind so different from that of an ordinary human being that the reasonable person would term it abnormal.

Grant's solicitor argued that with the statements of family and friends saying Grant was a calm, kind man who under duress just snapped into this other person, and because of the trauma he had experienced suffered dissociated amnesia. The doctors confirmed that Grant has never remembered what he actually did up to and during the trial.

The jury listened to the argument from both sides and retired to discuss the details they were given and conclude a verdict. It took the jury twenty four hours. The court was reconvened for the decision. A hush came over the court. Grant's son and daughter were present.

The judge asked if the jury had they reached a verdict. They said, "Yes, not guilty of voluntary manslaughter!"

Clark was met by Joe coming out of the court. Joe said to him, "Well, I did not expect that, surely it was a wrong decision. All the evidence pointed to him doing the murder."

Clark said, "On the evidence a jury of 12 people decided he was not guilty and that is why we have a justice system. Sometimes we might not agree with their decision and sometimes we agree. In fact I agree with them on this case."

Clark patted Joe on his back as they walked down the steps of the Court House.

UNFORGIVING

Chapter 1

They had been married for many years and lived in a leafy lane row of houses. A good area when you looked at the houses, which had the appearance of neat lawns and newly painted front doors. You could just picture them all out cutting their lawns on a Sunday, weather permitting. One could say, a normal suburban road, but behind closed doors things may be different.

This particular couple had lived in their house for some years now, were comfortably well off. They had no children so they had worked all their lives, had plenty of money to spend on themselves and their home. It was perfect until one summer's day when it all changed.

It was something small at first between them, that lit the fuse, slow burning. Things they had put up with all the time they had lived together.

She always put her clothes away, in colour, style and type in orderly racks. She was tidy when it came to clothes, in fact you could say she had OCD. Then when it came to shoes she was the opposite, they were left everywhere, so much so she could not find the right coloured ones to co-ordinate with the outfit sometimes. It would drive him mad, falling over them sometimes, but he bit his lip and was always helping her look for the right pair, upstairs and downstairs. But one day he had had enough and snapped.

"Why don't you file your shoes away like your clothes? I just don't understand you," he said.

She turned slowly, staring him directly in the eye and snorted, "Mind your own business, I never asked for your help to find my shoes did I?" She stood with her hands on her hips and looking defiant .

"Another thing, what about your clothes, all over the bedroom floor, which I have to pick up and put in the linen basket which you are too idle to do?" she replied.

He was getting mad now and slammed his fist onto the bedside table and walked out of the bedroom. She was not happy with him in any shape or form. He had to go, she was always right! She now realised that just maybe she had made a mistake and married him. How had she fallen in love with him?

Sarah remembered how they met, with fond memories some five years ago. Yes it was, she thought at the time, love at first sight. In fact it was a blind date. Her friend had set her up with him against her better judgement. She went, thinking it won't be that bad.

She was meeting her friend at a bar. When she walked in and saw there were a couple of men standing with her. Too late to turn round and go, she had to go with it. She approached the bar and the two men turned round. She knew Jerry, he was Sue's partner, it was the other guy standing there she assumed was her blind date. She sucked in air through her mouth, swallowed hard and walked towards them.

Sue introduced Richard to her and she said, "Hi, my name is Sarah, very nice to meet you."

Richard took her hand, and she thought he was going to shake it, but instead he brought it to his lips and kissed it. She was taken aback. A gentleman, she thought. Maybe this won't be too bad after all.

They all sat down to eat after getting drinks. The conversation between the four flowed, no awkward silence. It gave her a good feeling. Maybe it could work, time would tell.

Richard arranged to take Sarah to the theatre and out for meals, even to her favourite haunts which they both enjoyed. They could not believe the things they both liked. It was a match made in heaven or so they both believed.

Maybe it is true what people say when they say you never know someone until you live with them, and usually one in the partnership gives more than the other for it to truly work? Time would tell. Both Sarah and Harry had houses so they decided after a brief time to sell them both and buy a new one between them. This would be the dream house for her and he would go along with it. They set a date for the wedding and started looking for a house together.

Maybe she did not heed the warning signs when they were viewing properties together and just ignored them, he was the same. She wanted a dressing room, he wanted a large mature garden and a large kitchen as he loved to cook. She also wanted a study, so finding a house to suit both their needs took time. Location was important as their jobs for both of them were high powered ones, so not too far away to travel, would be good. So it took them six months before they found their ideal home in a leafy suburb with a tidy front garden.

Chapter 2

Sarah reflected, it seemed so long ago now but it wasn't really. They had fun along the road together but now things were grating on her. She was less forgiving of his ways. Her anger was growing like a poison polluting her body, turning her against him. She started having dark thoughts about getting rid of him and not just dumping him, murdering him! particularly when he verbally attacked her, but never physically. She pushed those thoughts away at first and then with time embraced her dark thoughts, so much so it started to change her character.

It was the friend who introduced her to Richard who noticed the changes. She would say, "That is not very nice to say about Richard." Sarah would brush it away by saying she did not really mean it. Then, with time, it got worse as she was always complaining about Richard more than praising him, so much so that her friend said, "I did tell you to live with each other first under one roof and you told me you did not need to as you knew each other." Sarah stormed out of the room, slamming the door behind her. Sue had hit a raw nerve.

Sarah hated being told she was wrong. It went against everything she believed in. She knew now she had to get rid of him, he was ruining her life, but how? She was not sure at this moment in time. Sinister thoughts filled her head. She was plotting to murder him to let him suffer, rather than walk away from him. She needed revenge on him for spoiling her life.

She needed to think hard about ways she could do it without being discovered. Poisoning him would be easy as it could be a mistake, like putting weed killer into a coke bottle. He loved his garden as well, so that might be the easy way to do it. He was always using weed killer on the dandelions!

Chapter 3

She was sitting out in the garden sun bathing, making the most of the summer weather at the time. He was weeding the garden beds. An idea came into her head.

"Richard, do you have any interesting books on plants and shrubs?" she asked.

"Why? You have never shown any interest before," he said.

"Well I was reading this book and it was saying a lot of gardens are full of poisonous plants and we are not aware of the potential dangers," she stated.

He turned and walked over to her, "Actually, that is a point. Maybe I should get a book and investigate what I have in the garden. You never know what I might find," he said.

She agreed with him, so it looked like he would be doing the work for her. She turned back to her book and took a sip of her wine from her glass and settled herself. He went back to weeding. She thought to herself this maybe easier than she thought, and she may even get away with it.

She tolerated him when they were together only because of her plan she was plotting. It was not long after that conversation in the garden about poisonous plants that one evening he showed her the book he had bought.

"Where did you get this book from?" she said as he handed it to her.

"That little book shop in the village. They have all sorts of quirky books," he said.

She flicked through the book and then said, handing it back to him, "Have you identified any plants and shrubs in our garden that are poisonous?"

"Not yet but it should not be a problem with this book," he said, sitting down and looking at the book with great interest.

She said, "Make sure you tell me which I shouldn't cut to go into vases as I don't want to get poisoned or ill."

He laughed, "As if I would."

She may have given him some warped idea to kill her! She made a nervous laugh. She thought this was going the wrong way and maybe she needs to act quicker just in case. She went back to watching her TV programme, glancing over to Richard every few minutes when he caught her glance and smiled.

"Do you want a drink?" she asks him.

"No thanks, I am fine," he said.

She got up and went to the kitchen and put the kettle on. She was panicking inside. What has she started? She needed to get hold of the book soon so she could decide what to do, otherwise it might have to be the weed killer!

The click of the kettle, now boiled, brought her thoughts back to now. She poured the water into her cup and stirred it and then took it into the lounge to continue watching her TV programme.

Richard was gone, probably gone to bed throwing his clothes on the floor everywhere just to annoy her. Maybe she could try leaving hers on the floor for once. No she tried that it lasted two days before it drove her crazy and she had to tidy them away. It was psychological warfare now between them.

He was pushing her to her limits to see how she would react. She had thrown things at him, but only soft items like socks, nothing hard yet. Sometimes he would push all her buttons and she would have to remove herself out of the room before she did something serious, but wait she was thinking of murdering him, that's serious stuff.

She sipped her coffee. Why was he doing this to her. Why did he not just leave her or did he want her to attack him so he could get the police involved. Was that how he was thinking? She was not sure how his mind worked. She went back to watching her programme and pushed those thoughts back to the recesses of her mind and sipped her coffee.

She had to wait for a few days before she managed to get her hands on the book. He had left it on the hall table and was away with work for a couple of days, just a conference in Edinburgh. So she grasped her chance to read the book that night. She would put the gym on hold so she could do some homework from the book. She noticed the notes he had started making and where they were left in the book. She needed to return them to the right place so he would not notice that she had used the book.

The notes were interesting to see what trees, shrubs and plants were poisonous and in their garden. She shuddered at the thought, as a chill ran down her spine. She read the list of what he had written so far: yew, rhododendron, laburnum, lily of the valley, Portuguese laurel all things he had found growing in the garden. She used the book and found each one and the write up of what part was poisonous and how toxic. The one she found interesting was the Portuguese laurel. It was only when it was cut and stored in a confined space that it gives off cyanide gas from the leaves, berries and branches.

She found that interesting. She looked at the picture of the shrub and thought that the berries would be the poisonous part of it. Maybe she could identify it in the garden then watch for him pruning it as he was always taking loads in the car to the recycling plant. Maybe it wouldn't be long before he took more in the car, therefore creating the gas in a confined space.

She needed to plan this carefully. She put his papers back in the book how she found them and placed it back on the hall table. She now had a plan.

Chapter 4

Richard came back from the conference full of himself. It was sickening really. She was just tolerating him with gritted teeth. She had come to hate this man, and the anger in her was so dark now. How had she changed so much? How could a man do this to her?

She put on her 'that's nice' face and exchanged a few words. He had met a couple of guys at the conference and they were going out Saturday night together. "That's fine," she said.

"I am going out as well," she replied. "Don't forget to get the gardening done on Saturday like you normally do," she added, knowing full well he would not have time to take the stuff to the recycle plant the same day and would have to do it Sunday.

Her plan was taking shape. The rest of the week soon went and come Saturday morning she decided to help him in the garden. He was surprised and welcomed the help. She put her scruffy clothes on and gardening gloves and went to join him.

"Shall I put the branches straight into the car to save some time?" she asked.

"No, you have to watch some of these trees and shrubs, I'll do it in the morning," he replied.

"You will be too hung over in the morning knowing you. I'll do it in the morning for you before you get up. Then after breakfast you can take it to the recycle plant," she insisted.

He nodded and continued working, cutting the branches of the Portuguese laurel. The small stuff was bagged but the larger branches she pulled along to the back of the garage where the path lead to the drive.

She would load the car tonight. He was getting a taxi, and not driving the car, as she was with the girls. Then the toxic fumes would have time to build up overnight and hopefully as he drove to the recycle plant, he would crash the car. She hoped it would be a quick death for him!

Her mind drifted back to the present as she heard him call her, "Are you with me?"

"Sorry, mind wandering on what I'm going to wear this evening. What next? Okay that one then," she replied. She needed to keep her mind on the job.

"Thanks for your help, Sarah. It does make a change from us always being at each other's throat," he said.

Sarah swallowed hard and said, "Yes, but it won't last, we both know one of us has to give in and it won't be me."

She took her gloves off and stormed off into the house. She went upstairs and decided she would draw herself a relaxing bath before tonight.

Richard continued for a little while longer in the garden, pulling the larger branches to the pile Sarah had already started. He paused as he put the last one on the pile, and picked up her gloves that she had thrown down before she went into the house. Looking at the gloves he thought do I actually love this angry person I am married to? She must really hate me. He snapped out of it and went back to clear the gardening things up and put them away in the garage before he went in to the house for a shower to get ready to go out.

Sarah was already out of the bathroom and in her bedroom. Yes separate rooms now. She just could not stand his mess any more. He did not like it but because he felt he was not messy, they never agreed

51

whose fault it was. It was easier this way.

He went to shower and get ready. They both ended up sitting in the lounge with a glass of wine before they got their taxis. Sarah had put music on but of course it was not to Richard's taste. He made comments about it, which she ignored. She thought not too long now, patience will be rewarded!

Richard's taxi arrived first, a toot from the taxi to make him aware it had arrived. He said to Sarah, "Enjoy your evening."

"Yes you too," she replied.

He shut the door behind him. She breathed a big sigh. Did she want to do this? She ran upstairs, changed her clothes and came down and out into the garden. She had another hour to do this. His car keys in her hand, she opened the back of the car. He had already dropped the back seats ready to load the branches.

She got her gloves out of the garage and started loading the branches into the car. It took her half an hour to do it and when she had finished she put the gloves back in the garage after locking the car. She went back into the house, went straight upstairs and changed ready to go out for the evening with the girls.

It was not long after that, her taxi arrived outside. She picked up her keys and went out the door for her night out in the bars in town.

Sarah got back first from her night out, before Richard did. She went straight to her bed as her feet were sore and she was thirsty. She went into the bathroom and drank a glass of water then filled another glass with water and took it to bed with her. Now they were sleeping in separate rooms she would not be disturbed by him when he got home but she needed to be up before him. She got into bed and switched the light off. She put her head on the pillow and was soon asleep.

Richard came in a lot later and a little worse for wear but managed to lock the door and get up the stairs safely before falling on the bed fully clothed, and he fell asleep, snoring.

Sarah woke at little after nine, and put her dressing gown on and went into his bedroom to see him lying fully clothed on the bed. She turned and walked out of the room and into her own. She slipped into the shower and let the water run over her face and body to revive her. She dried herself, dressed, then went down into the kitchen to start breakfast. It was a cooked one, the only way to help a hang-over, and the smell of cooking bacon would definitely wake him up.

Sure enough he walked into the kitchen, looking terrible, a lot worse for wear but the smell was too much for him to stay in bed. Over the years he found a cooked breakfast was the answer to a night out.

He sat at the table and drank the glass of water as well as orange juice that was put out for him. She refilled them both for him and went back to what she was doing, preparing his breakfast for them both. She put two eggs into the pan for him, once cooked put them onto his plate and along with bacon, sausages and tomatoes put the plate in front of him. The toaster popped up two slices of toast at that same moment so she put them on a plate as well and sat them down next to his other one.

Then she said, "And don't say I don't do anything for you. Now when you are finished you can take all the garden rubbish to the recycling plant seeing you need to get it done today."

He looked up, chewing, finishing his mouthful of

food, "Great then you can help me load the car when I come back down," he said.

"No, already done it this morning," she lied.

"I got up earlier than you and drank less when I went out," she said. She continued with cooking herself an egg which she put on her plate with some bacon for her breakfast and sat down to eat. She ate in silence.

After he had finished his breakfast he took a cup of coffee upstairs with him. He stood in the shower letting the warm spray soak over him. He felt human again and when he had finished in the shower, shaved and dried himself, then dressed. He felt more normal now. He came down and collected his car keys and called out to her he was off. He slammed the door.

In the kitchen Sarah was sat down slowly drinking her coffee and wondering what she had done. Was it true that the Portuguese laurel once cut and kept in a confined space gave off cyanide gas? She heard the car pull out of the drive. How long would it take to react to the gas? How far would he get to drive? Questions she could not answer.

She busied herself in the kitchen, clearing up after loading the dishwasher with breakfast things. She looked at the clock. Half an hour had passed. She would give it another half hour and then should she start worrying?

Chapter 5

The phone rang which woke her up, she must have nodded off watching catch up TV. She answered the telephone. It was a girlfriend she had gone out with last night. Her partner had rung to say that Richard's car had been in an accident. He was at the hospital and for her to come quick, he was in a bad way. She gasped, "Okay but which hospital? I'll come right away."

By the time she got to the hospital, sadly she found out he had died from his injuries. The police were there as well and wanted to speak to her once she had been to see Richard.

Her friend had picked her up to take her to the hospital as she was not in a fit state to drive herself, her friend pointed out. Her friend went into the cubicle with her to see him for support. The nursing staff and doctors could not have been more helpful to her. Even though she had planned it, she was still shocked by the reality of it all.

She was taken to a room and given a cup of tea with her friend. After a little while the police officer came in and sat down with her. He wanted to talk to her.

The officer said, "I know it must be a shock to you but we need to talk to you."

Sarah asked, "How did it happen? He was only going to the recycling place to take the garden rubbish."

The officer explained that when they found the vehicle it had hit a lamppost, with the car a wreck and fire and ambulance present on the scene. From what they gathered from eye witnesses, one minute he was in the outer lane of the dual carriageway the next he veered across the traffic and hit the lamppost. An eye witness said he had passed out at the wheel.

Sarah explained he had been out the night before, but had had a cooked breakfast that morning to make sure he was okay to drive. She went on to say no history of heart problems. They explained that they had taken bloods for tests to see whether he was over the limit or whether drugs were involved. They would release the body as soon as possible to her. She thanked them and was told she was free to go whenever she wanted. She finished her tea, spoke to the nurse and decided to go home with her friend. She had lots of thoughts going through her mind at that moment and she was not thinking straight.

Her friend, Sue said, "How you holding up? This has been a shock and hard to deal with no doubt?"

Sarah replied looking out of the window of the car, "I can't believe this is really happening, it seems like I am dreaming and hope to wake up and find he is still alive."

Sue replied back, "Don't worry I'll stay with you tonight, you don't have to talk."

She drove on in silence until they reached Sarah's house. They went into the house, and Sarah went to sit in the lounge while Sue went into the kitchen to make a cup of tea.

Sarah sighed, sitting on the sofa, feeling numb. Had it been her fault or was it the alcohol still in his system that made him lose concentration? She wouldn't know until the blood results from the police confirmed it, or not. She felt a cold shiver run up her spine just at the thought of it.

Sue came in with a tray of tea and put it down in front of her. They both picked up a mug of hot tea, a touch of sugar in Sarah's. They drank in silence for a while then Sue offered some papers the hospital had given her. Sarah looked down at them. They were how to deal with losing someone and the things you have to do. She looked up with a blank expression and said to Sue, "What do I do now," holding out the papers to give to her.

Sue took hold of them and sorted through, reading as she went along, then asked Sarah for a pad so she could write down each step. As she was doing this Sarah just slowly drank her tea. When Sue had finished reading everything and making notes she turned to Sarah.

"You have to do this part yourself. I'll be here but he was your husband and you will know what his wishes were for a funeral," Sue said.

Sarah turned to her, swallowed hard and said, "Yes, you're right I owe it to him to give him a good send off, and I need to contact the Solicitors for the will we made as well," she replied back.

Something had clicked in her she was now back on track, it was like a cog had turned in her brain, shutting the reality out and now was in practical mode. She looked at the list, then Sue and what she had planned. Then they made telephone calls for the rest of the day. They could do no more by early evening so they both cooked tea in the kitchen and ate. It was like Sarah was on automatic pilot.

Chapter 6

The Police contacted Sarah a week later to say that they had taken more samples of blood and tissue to send off for a toxicology report which would see if any alcohol and/or chemical substances were present. That would show if he had taken any drugs the night before. She argued that he would not do this but the officer said it would at least confirm that. The only thing was that the report would take six to eight weeks to come back. They were not prepared to release the body until the report was back. Sarah was stunned into silence. The officer was saying, "Are you still there Miss?" Sarah came to and replied, "Yes, sorry, I was a little stunned at what you said. He had never taken drugs knowingly, so why should you think that?"

The officer replied, "The post mortem showed he hadn't had a heart attack or clot to the brain, which ruled out a cause death before he crashed. We now have to look at other factors for his death, which we need to investigate further."

This was a normal procedure the officer explained and said they would be in touch with her when they had news of cause of death and releasing the body.

Sarah put the phone down and stared across the room in a trance. How was she to go forward with things? She could not if she had no body to bury and funeral to organise. Everything including her life was on hold. She needed to be busy she needed to work, she had to go back, surely it was the only way.

She picked up the phone and called her boss, explained the problems she had and that she wanted to come back to work until she could progress matters once the police had answers to her questions. Her boss was fine as he needed her back as soon as possible she was invaluable in the office. She put the telephone down and rang Sue, her friend, and explained what the police had told her. She seemed to understand what she was saying until the drugs were mentioned.

"Are the police indicating that he may have taken drugs? Jerry was with him most of time that night and I am sure he would have mentioned it," Sue said.

"I am sure none of the guys are implicated unless traces of substances are found but surely they are not?" Sue asked.

This was getting complicated and she needed to finish this conversation before it got too heavy. Sarah said she would be in touch as soon as she knew something, and put the telephone down. What was she to do? Concentrate on going back to work, that would take her mind off things.

The next few weeks she switched onto automatic pilot and got on with things as best she could in the circumstances, dreading her telephone ringing in case it was the police and what they had discovered. She would get up in the mornings and when she was dressed, walk into his bedroom. It was strange looking around the room, looking at his clothes, watches and everything of his. It reminded her of his existence. She found it difficult to deal with things as she thought before he died she would find it easy to get rid of his things. But now reality hit home and she found it pulling at her heart. She realised she loved him at first, very much, but the feuding gave her a bitter taste in her mouth.

She walked out of the room and downstairs into the kitchen. Again as she sat eating her breakfast looking around, items kept reminding her of him. He was the cook and in the early days he would cook superb meals for her in the evenings and at weekends. She missed his cooking and his little touches he used to do like a rose on the serviette, a ring in her glass of fizz and more, but these were the only ones that stuck in her mind.

She got up and put her bowl in the dishwasher. She grabbed her keys and handbag and walked out the door, turning, looking back inside the house, this perfect house they chose together. Her dreams were now shattered and it lay heavy on her shoulders. The guilt. It was her fault.

She worked hard at work, pushing her thoughts of what she had done away. She went on like this each day, until she broke down one morning before setting off for work. She burst into tears. It was like a wave of grief had engulfed her and she had no control over her emotions, the tears flooded from her like a waterfall. She wanted to turn the tap off to stop it but had no physical control.

She needed to telephone work, as there was no way she could work with the way her emotions were behaving. She rang her boss and through the sobs and sniffing was reassured that it was fine and to come in when she felt she could handle work.

She fell back on the settee, relieved in one way, but she was being sucked into this dark pit, not seeing any way out. She buried her head in her hands and cried. She was not sure how long she was like that but when she lifted her head from her hands, her lap looked wet from the tears that dripped through her fingers.

She wiped her face and blew her nose. She needed a drink, a stiff one. Maybe a whisky and water would help. She got up and poured herself a drink. That went down in one go, then another. She felt a warm glow as she put the empty glass down on the table. She needed to have more to make the pain go away! By the time she had finished drinking, what was that her fourth or sixth? She was drunk and lay on the settee, crying again now. The drink had made her more depressed and had not helped. She cried herself to sleep.

Several hours had passed when she was woken by the doorbell ringing and someone banging on the door. She slowly lifted her head, which was fuzzy and thumping with a headache. She dragged herself up to the door, opened it, and there stood a very concerned looking Sue.

"Sarah, are you okay? I was so concerned as you never answered the telephone and when you did not come to the door, I got really scared," she said.

Sarah replied in a shaky voice, "Yeah, really sorry."

Sue came in, catching Sarah, who was unsteady on her feet, and guided her back to the settee, then spotted the half empty bottle of whisky on the table. Sue decided to put her down to sleep it off on the settee. Then went and got a blanket to go over her, settled her down and she was back to sleep in minutes. Sue sat on the chair opposite her looking concerned. What had happened to push her to drink? Was it just grief? Can it do that to you? She had no experience of losing someone so close like Sarah.

Sue decided to speak to her mum who was great on advice and had seen a lot in her life. She telephoned her while Sarah slept, speaking softly to her mum explaining about what she had found. Her mum said there was no rule book for grief and that everyone handles it differently and all she can do is be there for Sarah. The drinking is a crutch but Sue must be aware it can get out of hand if not checked. So as much support as possible in every way possible to see her through this.

Sue put the telephone down and cleared the bottle and glasses away. She found a lemon in the kitchen and made a hot water and lemon drink and brought it ready for Sarah to drink when she woke.

She settled down to watching Sarah breathing slowly and quietly, waiting for her to wake from her alcoholic haze.

Chapter 7

Sarah woke at tea time. She felt ill, with a dry mouth and a terrible headache. Sue came to the rescue with glasses of water, tablets and a hot water with lemon, as well. After half an hour she felt a little more normal but was feeling guilty about what she had done. They talked, Sarah cried more but now realised she was grieving for Richard and it was a natural process. They talked more and knew she had to take a step at a time. Sarah wanted to collect the items from downstairs that were his and take them to his room and when she was ready to deal with them all she would. A small step at a time.

Sue would sleep and stay with her. They went out for walks and the gym when she felt she could do it. She believed she would come out the other side a wiser person. She had the burden of feeling guilty at what she had done which she would have to live with forever. She would see what the police found and then go forward from that evidence they found.

Sue was a miracle that had picked up the shattered pieces and put them back together. She was a rock and kept her off the bottle, which she knew she could turn to quite easily. The days passed, and Sue decided she would only come in the evenings for dinner, to see how she was coping during the day. This after they had removed the objects from everywhere that reminded her of him and put them in his room.

The days went well with Sarah going out for walks, shopping and coffee. The crying had reduced and she felt better, not as depressed, which was good as she did not want to ask the doctor for medication for it.

One day after several weeks, Sara said, "I think I am ready to go back to work, I feel I can cope now."

So the next day she returned to work feeling in charge of her emotions once again. She had only been back at work for a week when the police contacted her and asked if she could call in to see an officer at the station. She rang Sue and asked her to come with her.

They both drove their cars to the police station and walked in and asked for the officer dealing with the case.

They were shown into a room. Sarah was quietly thinking she must show surprise and shock whatever they found. A few seconds later the officer who introduced himself, as Officer George Scott, who had been dealing with the case, came into the room. They now had the toxicology report back and they were expecting some things to show but not others.

Sue and Sarah looked at each other and held hands tightly. He went on to say that the alcohol level was over the 80 milligrammes of alcohol per 100 millilitres of blood which from the information they had was not surprising. They also found traces of other drugs which indicated he had taken Ecstasy the night before. Sarah gasped, "I had no idea he would do that, so silly." She dabbed at a tear rolling down her cheek. He asked was she okay for him to continue and she nodded. He went on to say they also found cyanide which was strange until they looked at what he was carrying in the car at the time of the accident. The cuttings of Portuguese laurel which he was transporting gave off gases when cut and stored in enclosed space, which on top of everything else would have rendered him unconscious at the wheel, which then caused the car to cash into the lamp post.

By this time Sarah could not help herself but cry. Sue comforted her and the officer apologised for upsetting her, but he required details on the drug taking. Sue interjected and said she would give the name of the clubs and bars they went to, but none of the guys he was with saw him with anything in their company. The officer thanked her for her help.

"I am sorry for the delay but we had to be sure what made him lose consciousness and I would say a combination of factors. We will get a death certificate issued and release the body now. Which funeral director are you using or you can get them to contact us?" he said, passing over a card to her.

Once Sarah composed herself again they stood up, thanked the officer and were shown out of the office and station. They went to their cars and Sue followed Sarah home. When they arrived they walked in and Sue headed to the kitchen to make a cup of tea for them. Sarah went and sat down to take in what had been said to them.

Sarah said, "I cannot believe he would be silly enough to do drugs."

Sue replied, "Well the guys he went with said that if he wanted to he could have bought them when he went to the toilet, as a couple of them said they were approached in a couple of the bars they visited."

Sarah sighed and said, "Why would he though? Was he unhappy with me? Do you think? Did I push him that way?"

Sue reassured her it had nothing to do with her. They then started to talk about what to do next. They had made a start by letting people know he had died but now she needed the funeral director to make the arrangements so his body could be picked up and a date arranged for the service he would want.

They talked for some time, getting advice from Sue's mum who guided them along. Sarah rang the funeral director she had decided upon, talked to them, and they were extremely helpful. She arranged for them to call the next day to organise things and they needed to make sure she had the death certificate to progress things. So Sarah rang the police contact number and spoke to someone. They said they would give the death certificate to the funeral director when they collected the body. She thanked them and put the telephone down. Now she would wait for tomorrow. In the meantime Sarah and Sue discussed what sort of service to arrange.

Sarah and Richard had not discussed funerals. Why would they at such a young age? So she had no idea whether he was religious or not. So they both decided on a non- religious service with just someone talking about his life. It would be hard as he lost both of his parents at a very young age and was brought up by his grandmother who died when he was twenty two. He had such a sad history.

Sue and Sarah wrote some notes down and wrote some of his favourite songs he liked. When they were finished they felt drained. Sue offered to stay the night which Sarah was grateful for so they both went to bed early after a light tea.

The next day the funeral director came. They talked, being guided about things for the day, time, place etc. All she had to do now was contact people with details. The wake venue was decided as well so people could choose whether to attend both or not.

Chapter 8

The day had arrived of the funeral. Sarah was nervous and emotional and was glad Sue and Jerry were there to support her.

The hearse arrived with a car following behind. Sarah was acting as if it was all a dream seeing the coffin. She went through the motions at the chapel within the crematorium and Jerry gave a wonderful speech about Richard's life. Afterwards strangers came up to her saying they were sorry for her loss but in her deepest thoughts she was wishing she had not done what she did.

Sue and Jerry ushered her to the car to go to the place where they were having refreshments. When they arrived Sue made sure she drank diet coke and kept an eye on her.

Looking around the room at all these strange faces, she found herself drawn to someone, she was sure she knew him but could not remember his name. He looked up and caught her eye and patted the chair next to him for her to join him. She went over mesmerised by his hazel eyes and clean cut look.

"Hi, I'm Sam. I worked with Richard a lot of years. He talked about you a lot, so much so I think I really know you," he said.

Sarah smiled and said, "Yes. Sam, Richard did mention you as a work colleague and how you worked on projects together over the years."

Sam talked, and looked after her, getting her a drink and food. He pointed out people around the room, who they had both worked with. They found it easy to talk to each other, no silent moments that can be awkward.

Sarah went to the ladies room. She looked into the mirror at herself and thought, no you cannot do this to yourself, you have just buried your husband but she really found herself attracted to Sam and if she allowed it, it could go well this time. She would make sure it was different, she hoped.

FORBIDDEN LOVE

Chapter 1

She sat in the village café drinking her coffee and as she glanced around the room her eyes stopped at a man sitting with a smartly dressed lady in a suit. It was the man who looked familiar to her but she did not know why. She glanced away and drank her coffee, at the same time delved into the recesses of her brain for the name of the man, she thought she had recognised.

After a short while he got up and left with the woman but glanced over to Emily, catching her eyes as he turned to leave. She gave a sharp intake of breath and looked away. She must have known him for her to react like that, she thought. Maybe in the recesses of her mind the information was filed away, but how to access it?

She stood up and went to pay for her coffee and left the café, closing the door as she stepped out onto the pavement. The sun was bright in her eyes that morning, it reminded her of something but she could not remember. She put on her sunglasses, turned, and walked in the opposite direction to the man and woman she thought she knew. Where was she going, she thought to herself. Home of course. Driving? Yes silly, now where was the car?

She collected her thoughts and walked towards the car park and there was her yellow Mini. It was old by modern standards, but she loved it. She got her key out of her handbag and opened the door the old fashioned way, with a key! She got into the driver's seat, flung her bag onto the passenger seat and put her key in the ignition. She turned the key and the engine started. She loved the throaty noise of the engine.

It was her father's love of old cars. When he used to tinker with the cars, he showed her under the bonnet one day, and she was hooked. She had had old MG's, E Types but she loved her old Mini. She knew every part under the bonnet, not like modern cars. Modern cars had too much electronic stuff under the bonnet now and she hated that.

She drove home and put her pride and joy away in her garage and let herself into her house. She set down her bag and keys and went into the kitchen to make a cup of tea. Waiting for the kettle to boil, she sat for a minute in deep thought, then said out loud to herself, "Who was that man in the café? I am sure I know him from my past job."

The kettle clicked off. She rose to make her tea still thinking, she still knew him, then dismissed the thought as being silly and made her tea. She sat down with her tea, sipping it and looking at the local paper, when she spotted a story that caught her eye.

A person, who was not named, had died under suspicious circumstances. The police were baffled and were investigating further. She read on with interest. She was intrigued by the case. Why, she was not sure, but she knew from instinct that there was more to the case.

Emily had worked for MI6 for a lot of years as an operative. She had never married or had any children. It was on her last mission that the damage was done. She received a very bad head injury which started to affect her memory, so much so they could not let her return to work.

Her long term memory was being affected slowly, but not her short term memory. She was aware there was something happening but she dismissed it. Everyone forgot things she would tell herself. She had two cats to keep her company, or should she say when they felt like keeping her company! They were semi feral and so they would only come into the house on their terms.

She went back to the paper and read more articles and then checked on share prices. She had bought a few with the lump sum they had given her when she had to retire through ill health. But as she always reminded herself, you never retire from MI6.

She enjoyed working for the Secret Intelligent Service. She was responsible for gathering intelligence outside the UK in support of the government's security, defence, foreign and economic policies. Well actually she was involved with the security side. She travelled the world wherever she was needed, but was based at the MI6 building on Albert Embankment in Vauxhall, London.

She loved her job and was disappointed when they said she was unfit to continue in the field after the accident. They did offer her an office job, but she enjoyed the freedom of the job she did with all the travelling to different countries around the world. She had now settled into the village life nicely as she felt she needed to rediscover another life. She was painting and drawing and had set up a website under another name to inspire other artists and to sell her art. She did not go to shows or exhibitions, as she wanted to keep herself out of the lime light as much as possible.

Yes, Emily could feel a certain amount of contentment, but still yearned for the thrill of being out in the field, not just using her own abilities but sometimes working as a team. She put down the newspaper now and went to the computer. She needed to send an email to her old friend she had worked with about the article she had read. She knew it was hiding something of importance but not sure what. It was her instinct.

She went to her study and sat at her desk. She opened the computer and sent the email to an address that was secure but she would use her code words when sending it, as it was becoming more difficult in today's technology to send something secure. They had, after she had left MI6, started employing computer buffs to stop cyber- attacks from outside.

She started typing…

Hi, thought you would like to know the weather is fine but think a storm may be brewing your way. Wondered if I could help in case it did some damage and you needed my helping hands?
Miles

She pressed the send button. She thought to herself, hope that was not too cryptic for them. She switched the computer off and headed to her studio where her painting was done. She was finishing a watercolour picture of some flowers she had started and just needed another hour's work to finish it. She settled into painting, her thoughts completely calming her so she was in her 'zone'. She took a few minutes to realise that someone was knocking on the door of her house. She glanced up at the clock. It would be her food shopping order. She put her paint brushes down and hurried to the door. Upon opening it, there was the delivery guy waiting with one of her baskets. She waved him in, following behind. He set it down while he went for the next one. She had emptied it by the time he came back with the next one, the fresh produce. He helped her unpack it and they chatted as always.

Simon had become known to her over the months she had started getting home deliveries and he had shown interest in her paintings so much so he had commissioned her to do a painting of certain flowers for his mother's birthday. Today he was picking it up. She showed him into the studio where she painted and he whistled when he saw all her canvases.

Simon said, "That's amazing, how many do you sell?"

Emily replied, "Not enough, but then I have a run and sell 10, it just depends. Here is the one for your mother. I did not frame it as I was not sure how she would like it displayed. People do just hang canvases."

He thanked her and gave her the money for it and thanked her again saying his mother would be over the moon when she saw it. She showed him out and as he left she shut the door and secured it. Then she went back to the kitchen to put her groceries away. She put on some music as she walked through the lounge to the kitchen. She was humming away to herself when she suddenly stopped.

She said, "I knew I recognised that guy in the café, he was an operative I worked with in MI6. Why was he in the village? To spy on me? Or to keep an eye on me? Am I in danger perhaps?" She needed to make a telephone call.

Chapter 2

She put the telephone down after having a conversation with, shall we say Agent 416, as Emily was used to no names, especially on the telephone. She had an interesting conversation which filled in a few gaps for her. She was right in recognising the person she spotted in the café as an operative she had worked with. Her memory was not bad considering. Anyway, they were keeping an eye on her. She enquired with the Agent, was her life in any danger? They were on alert after the incident in the paper which Agent 416 would not go into detail about at this moment. She had to accept the answers. All he said was that they would be in touch.

She sat down gathering her thoughts. At least they were watching is case someone tried to get at her. But, she thought, do they want information from her or did they want to kill her? She would have to be patient as MI6 would feed her information only on a need to know basis. She would have to be ready to leave for a safe house at short notice she thought.

After lunch she went to pack a case ready, just in case. She wanted to be ready for anything. She went round the house checking windows and doors were locked firmly. She set her security alarm to notify her of anyone trying doors and windows which was connected to her watch. She noticed the email she sent earlier had been replied to, via her watch.

She made a quick sandwich and took it with her to the study. She put it down, took a mouthful and opened her computer. She saw the email, clicked on it and opened it up. She still had contacts in MI6 who would talk to her as others would not. She read it, it was in code.

Hi Miles,
Yes a storm is brewing and it may come your way and spoil the lovely weather you no doubt are having. I would batter down and close the shutters securely as it may cause property and personal damage. Can't say whether it is a hurricane or a cyclone but I would listen to the weather reports.
Reginald

She sat back in her chair, reached out for her sandwich and took a bite, chewing slowly, digesting both the sandwich and the message at the same time. She thought that it looked like all hell would be let loose soon. Wonder what it is all about? No use guessing, she thought, she would have to be patient and wait, not one of her attributes.

Emily shut the computer down, checked her watch and then decided to chill by painting. She picked up her plate and walked to the kitchen, put the plate down, poured herself a glass of water and went into her studio. She sat for a while looking at the blank canvas when a vivid picture appeared in her mind. It was a memory of an assignment. She imagined the square, the fountain, but his face, staring at her! She was overwhelmed to pick up the paint brush, she just had to paint what she was seeing. She had never done anything like this before. The brush seemed to have a life of its own and an urgency before the memory faded. It took an hour. She finished it and it was his eyes that made her shiver and feel cold. Why this memory and why now? She could not understand now but maybe in days to come she might remember the mission she was on when she found him in the square at one of the cafés.

She would wait for it to dry and then store it among her other paintings. She must not think about it, why, she was not sure at this stage.

She rinsed her brushes, dried them and then put them down in their usual place. She then went off to the kitchen to get another drink. She did herself a tray of tea and took it through to the lounge and sat down, putting the TV on for the news, actually the news channel itself. Nothing about the item in the newspaper was mentioned, she would have to bide her time. Something was brewing and it was not just her tea. She poured herself a cup and decided to watch a programme instead. But nothing took her fancy so she ended up watching a film.

When she looked at the clock after the film had finished, and she did not realise how late it was. She switched off the TV and checked everything, double checking that the security was set and went upstairs to bed, hopefully for a good night's sleep. She got into bed after folding her clothes up and decided not to read, but to go to sleep straight away. So she pulled the sheets up to her face, switched the light off, turned onto her side and it was not long before she was asleep.

Chapter 3

She woke the next morning, sunlight streaming through the window. She never bothered with an alarm clock these days. She sat up hoping today would be a good day for her. She went and had a shower, washed her hair, got dressed then dried her hair. It was when she sat down putting her make-up on, she looked at her watch. It was flashing. A sensor had been triggered in an area of the house. She thought it was strange that the alarm had not alerted her to this, but it may have only been someone trying to enter via a window. She finished and went to investigate downstairs.

It was alerting her to a window in the lounge, so went to look at it. She reset the security then rattled the window and the light lit up to alert her. Maybe someone tried to force entry and gave up? She dismissed it and walked into the kitchen.

She made herself some breakfast and a coffee and sat down. Picking up the TV remote, she switched it on to see if anything new had appeared in the news. Although she thought to herself that if it was too important to UK security they would have pulled the story from the media as soon as possible.

She ate her toast, deep in thought, when a knock came at the door. It caught her off guard a little and she jumped at the sound. Dismissing this as not coming from her door, another knock came again, louder this time. She rose from the table and walked to the door. Slightly apprehensively she looked through the peep hole to see who it was.

It was the postman with a parcel. She opened the door with the safety chain on just in case.

"Yes, can I help you?" she said.

"Parcel for you, and I need a signature please," the postman said, getting his electronic signature pad out.

She closed the door, took the chain off and opened the door. She signed and then he handed her the package. Glancing up the road at the same time, she saw his van parked but past that she noticed a small white van with indecipherable writing on the side. One of these delivery services she thought, and shut the door on the receding postman.

She was curious as to what was in the parcel. She had not ordered anything recently, she was sure of that. She took it into the kitchen put it down to inspect it first. Nothing pointed to where it had come from, the label was typed not hand written and it was her other name she went with now. She turned it over. There it was. With her trained eye, she spotted the tiny stamp mark 'M'. That was all she needed to know. She opened it with interest.

There was a typed note, a couple of photographs. She read the note. Yes, she was right, it was an informal but informative message. Looked like her past was about to take over her life. She always had this dark feeling that it might catch up with her. She had upset a lot of people along the way. She was very good at her job and captured and exposed a few people in the years she worked for MI6. Now her past was coming back to haunt her.

She turned her attention to the two photos. The first one was from a distance, her getting into her mini, but also in the picture a guy with a camera in a car, which looked like he was taking pictures of her, but she could not quite see his face. The second photo was the close up of his face. Although grainy, you could see his features but not his eyes.

She had the same feeling at seeing this photograph as she had when she was painting the picture of the square, fountain and cafés, then his face. Where was that place? She needed to remember. It would come to her when she was not thinking about it. She now knew she was being watched, but also her colleagues were also out there to look out for her. She liked working alone sometimes, but at other times it was good someone had your back.

No doubt now, she would be contacted and she would have to be ready to move at short notice. She had outside shutters fitted to the house for when she worked away, so the house would be secure when she left.

She pushed the note and the two photographs back into the envelope and discarded the box it had been put in. She put the kettle on. She needed a drink now, a strong coffee better than a whisky at this time of the morning. She walked towards her studio while the kettle boiled and looked at her paintings and equipment. Something was different. The brushes were out of place. She always put them in order of size and now looking at them they were not. The hairs on the back of her neck stood up, indicating that just maybe she was not alone.

'Think, Think', she told herself. Is there anything else out of place. She cast her eyes around the studio, she was so methodical and tidy, sure something would look out of place apart from the brushes. Yes, someone had touched the tubes of acrylic paint and a small canvas was on her easel. She slowly walked towards it, and gasped when she saw it.

He had painted an eye and the words 'watching you' on the canvas. He had been here but not set the alarm off! He must have used an electronic device to scramble the signal to allow him in and out quickly. Was it to scare her or warn her he was after her, to what ends? Revenge for what she did to him? Would he stoop so low as to kill her this time?

Now it came to her, the mission. He was a security risk, Enzo that was his name. He was an Italian who worked for the Mafia or the Sicillian Mafia at the time of her investigations. There were problems reported that they were infiltrating into the UK and MI6 wanted to stop them before they involved themselves with crime gangs and drugs which was already happening in the UK. Enzo had been identified and at first it was following and reporting on his activities. Then it became a bigger operation, and her objective was to get close to him while the others in the team acted as a gang that wanted some of the action with the Mafia.

That was her first meeting with him at Piazza Navona, Rome. She had looked up the details of the place in the tourist book, it stated that the plaza's oval shape was the only reminder of its origins as a Roman chariot track, but it remained a hub for both locals and visitors. The fountain, square and cafés as she remembered it had artists and street vendors as well. It was lively, lots of people about, tourists, locals and some wealthy people too. It was a good place to meet him. She was sitting drinking coffee waiting for him to appear for their meeting. He took up a table opposite hers, but facing her. It was as if he knew but those eyes, so dark, so searching as if he was looking inside her soul.

She gave a shiver, looking at the eye he had painted and remembering him. She went and checked the painting she had done of the memory. No, he had not found it. She needed to check in to let them know what her 'now' situation was. It was more urgent to get her out now as she was vulnerable. She looked at her watch and found the right section she needed, her glasses perched on the end of her nose to see, and pressed it. She would wait.

She needed to take the envelope upstairs and put it in her case, take her papers and gun out of the safe and stow them in the case as well. She needed then to take the case downstairs and wait. She did all this and ended up downstairs in the hall. She headed for the lounge and poured herself a large drink of whisky and soda and sat in the chair waiting. She stared at the front door, waiting for something, she did not know what. She stood up and went over to lower the shutters on everything except the front door. She sat down again, sipping her drink as she waited calmly for something to happen.

Chapter 4

Her watch made a noise, so she put on her glasses and looked down, mumbling to herself that she must get her contacts checked. They would be here in ten minutes to pick her up. She acknowledged the message and hoped Enzo was not waiting as well to either kill her or kidnap her to take her back to Italy. She had made some people in the Mafia unhappy when she uncovered the gang who were involved with smuggling drugs into the UK on a large scale. Emily and her team had really infiltrated the gang so much it was easy when they were ready to expose them. They managed to get them arrested red handed with the drugs. They were jailed, some in Italy, which with their judicial system was surprising. They were sent down for up to ten years but Enzo managed, with the help of his lawyer to get a lighter sentence.

He had promised her that was not the last time she would see him. No doubt, he would have been disappointed to find out she had retired, but that may have made it easier for him to find her, now out from under the MI6 umbrella.

Her watch bleeped and she went to her door, checked through the spyhole and saw it was Jason, yes that was his name, the one in the café with a lady she did not recognise.

She opened the door to him, "Hi, Jason. Comforting to see you. What is the plan?"

Jason replied, "To get you to a safe house so Enzo can't get to you. Then decide what the next step is, if you want to end this."

Emily smiled, "That sounds a good plan."

She reached down for her case in the hall and

walked out of the door, turning to lock it and to set the security on the house. Jason took her case off her. She was led to a large black car with blacked out windows which she got in and shut the door, feeling a little safer now.

They drove in silence, but after a short while she said, "How long has Enzo been out of jail?"

Jason replied, "Three months, but we only spotted him around your village in the last month. We think maybe he was going to kidnap you rather than kill you here, probably taking you back to Italy. This is as much as we have from intelligence as he has been flying below the radar a lot, which makes it more difficult to follow."

Emily replied, "Do you think he has been dealing with criminal gangs in the UK to get his information?"

"Yes," Jason replied and went on to say, "We think he has several contacts, different to before when we met him. We think the Mafia may have pushed him out and he has joined another group. That's what our intelligence has come back to say."

Emily said, "You can never get away from your past in this business. Never mind, lots to concentrate on now."

Jason nodded, he handed her a bottle of water, which she opened and drank from. She would sit back and try and relax and hope Jason and the team had a plan to pull Enzo out into the open so they had a chance of catching him.

She must have nodded off. She woke up with a start as they were driving through electric gates to some large property. She was sure she knew where she was, but could not at this moment in time remember.

She straightened herself up as Jason pulled up on the gravel drive to outside the front door of a manor house. Jason turned off the engine and got out to get Emily's case. As she opened her door to get out she looked up at the house. Where was she? She knew but it was buried deep in her brain, somewhere the memory. It would come to her, she thought, in time, hopefully before she was told.

She followed Jason, as the door was opened for them by a butler, yes now it came back to her. She had been here to recuperate after her accident, when an agent had offered her the use of it. She was waited on hand and foot, it was heaven and so was the food. Now she remembered it was called Hamland Manor, yes of course, it all came back to her.

She was shown into the lounge where her old boss from MI6 was waiting. He stood up, took her hand and kissed it then brought her near to him and embraced her. She pulled back and looked him up and down, then said, "My you look well, and not retired yet? That young wife of yours must be keeping you on your toes." They both laughed and he embraced her again.

As they separated he said, "Emily, you are looking well considering the accident, but how do you feel? I am so sorry to get you involved with Enzo but everything points to him going for you, no matter what. We will work this out, so you are safe."

She half laughed. "That will not happen, Charles, and you know it. I will have to be the bait so you can finish him, it is the only way. Or I go after him with my old team if you will allow me. Or do you have a plan?"

Charles looked at Jason, then back at Emily and said, "Well we thought you would not want anything to do with us, but if you feel up to it we shall see. We might have to get clearance for you though."

Emily smiled and said, "You don't have to go with my plan, but do you want to hear what I have in mind?"

Charles said, "I am listening."

Emily said first of all she would message her neighbour to feed the cats, as she had to leave suddenly as a relative was ill, and would be coming back in a couple of days with her relatives' son for a break. That way she could get an agent into the property with her for support.

"If Enzo has been watching the house and me like you said he may use the neighbour. She is a bit of a nosey neighbour and that is why I feed her information."

Emily was not sure if Jason had been recognised around the village by Enzo so she requested a younger guy from the team who knew her.

Charles said, "Can't see a problem, but what about a helper around the house or would that be too many people?"

Well it might look too much Emily thought, and said she could get some workmen working on the house guttering perhaps. In fact they talked about all sorts of tricks to make sure she would be safe, but not to make it look too unnatural that it would be noticed.

Coffee was brought in while they talked. When they felt they had put enough ideas in the melting pot for someone to sort, Emily excused herself. She felt tired and had not foreseen it would take so much out of her since the accident. Charles said he would arrange for a tray to be sent up to her room. She thanked him and left the room.

After she left the room Charles turned to Jason and

said, "Do you think she will be able to cope with the pressure, knowing Enzo is after her and probably want to either kidnap or kill her?"

Jason replied, "I think he wants to take her to Italy, not kill her in the UK. He fell in love with her I think, but I'm not sure if she rebuffed him. I think he will use his contacts in the UK to help him fly her home so he can keep her captive. To what ends I am not sure. Whether he will do it over land or air, depends on his contacts here. Either way I hope she is strong enough to be prepared for whatever gets thrown at her."

Jason went on to say, "Maybe it was not my place to say Enzo had romantic ideas about her."

Charles looked puzzled by what Jason had said, "I believe from the debriefing it was business as usual for her and no mention or hint of her feelings for him. Now go get your man without too many dead bodies along the way if you can."

Jason said, "Fine it was just that watching them together there was definitely something between them, but maybe I was mistaken."

The butler came in and said dinner was served. Charles asked for a tray to be sent up to Emily's room as she was not joining them. Charles thanked him and they both walked into the dining room for what smelt like a delicious meal, as always.

Chapter 5

After several days Emily went back home with her relatives' son, Daniel. Daniel had been on her team and someone she was happy with. He drove a hire car to take them to her house.

When she arrived her neighbour came round and introduced herself to Daniel. Emily did the same, stating that he was staying for a short holiday with her as he wanted to develop his painting skills. They chatted for a few moments and then Daniel said that they needed to go in. The neighbour agreed, apologising for holding them up.

She stopped and turned and said, "A very nice gentleman called looking for you, foreign accent. So not knowing what to say to him I suggested he come back next week."

Emily told her not to worry and that he had telephoned her so there was no problem. That was a lie of course, but it must have been Enzo nosing around the place. Emily opened her door, took the security off and opened the shutters and then reset the security via her watch. By that time Daniel had brought the cases in along with bags of food for them.

She showed him the kitchen and he set to putting the items away. She went to her study, opened the cabinet and checked the CCTV, which was all hidden in the bird boxes around the house outside. The grounds had some tall trees which made the positioning of the boxes easy. She watched the tapes. Yes a car drives up the drive, a man, yes Enzo. He knocked on her front door, then went next door, coming back later to his car and drove off. She resets the system to alert her to any movement outside and for the alert to be directed to her watch.

She went to the kitchen where Daniel was. He had put everything away and had made both of them a sandwich for lunch.

He said, "Tea or coffee, Miles?"

Emily replied. "Tea, but please call me Emily, especially in this environment, less suspicious and you need to practise."

Daniel smiled to himself. They had worked a lot together, and he liked her. She sat down as he brought the tea over with the sandwich. She took a bite of her sandwich, chewed a couple of times, swallowed and said, "We need to decide how we are going to do this. We agree it will be at night he will come, under the cover of darkness." Daniel nodded.

"Right, before Enzo went into the studio, he overrode the security somehow without triggering the whole system. I have double checked but now I have reprogrammed it to allow entry but to notify fully if we have a breach. That way we will be on alert. We will take it in turns to keep watch overnight," Emily said, then took another bite of her sandwich.

Daniel put on the table the small devices they needed to wear, so they could alert each other wherever they were in the house.

Emily said, "These are better than the ones I remember."

Daniel laughed. "Advancement in technology changes from week to week. These are more upgraded than you have been used to in the past."

Daniel thought, we are on our own, is this enough? But back up will not be far away. He checked his gun and asked where Emily's was, she said upstairs in her bag. She must get it out and make sure she put it somewhere handy.

After they had finished their lunch Emily took Daniel into her studio. He was impressed at the quality of her work, then stopped and pulled one piece out. "That was the Piazza Navona, Rome where you first met Enzo. How did you paint so much detail from so long ago?"

Emily came over to Daniel who was holding the painting. She shrugged her shoulders, "I had this flashback and needed to paint it and that is the finished picture. I know it is a bit scary looking at the detail and his eyes!"

She pulled out the one Enzo had left. Daniel was taken aback, "How did he know? Was there anything going on between you two, as it was always a question I never asked."

Emily was surprised by the question and said, "Yes I had to get close for the operation but when you have eyes that look into your soul, it is difficult not to fall for someone. But it was a job, so I had to be a little detached."

She now felt awkward and asked Daniel to sit at the easel and started him off painting something simple to try. She decided to go outside, remotely opened the door and picked up her scissors as she stepped out. She cut a few flowers and interesting grasses. She came back in and placed them on a white cloth. Happy she turned to Daniel, "Now paint what you see or if you prefer draw first then paint, up to you how you do it," Daniel laughed and picked up a pencil.

Emily got up as Daniel turned his head and said, "You are not going to oversee what I do."

Emily replied, "No, just enjoy yourself."

She left him and went off into the kitchen where she planned what to do for dinner for them. No alcohol for either of them, they needed clear heads. Emily had her suspicions that Enzo would strike sooner rather than later. Daniel called her to the studio as she was preparing the vegetables. She put down the knife and went into the studio to see what Daniel had achieved so far.

She looked at the sketch and his first lot of colour on the paper. She nodded, "Very good, you should take it up as a hobby and develop on it. Are you enjoying it?"

Daniel replied, "Yes, very relaxing, but I really should stop for now."

Emily smiled, "Dinner will be another twenty minutes, that's fine."

She left him to it. She turned, and noticed her watch flashed once. Oh no a security breach, damn, she thought. Turning to Daniel, she cleared her throat and as she turned towards him tapped her watch. He nodded.

Emily then returned to the kitchen as if nothing had happened, with Daniel following her once he had put the brushes down. He stood and drew his weapon.

Emily was caught off guard as Enzo grabbed her, knife to her throat, his mouth close to her ear, "Quiet, not a word, I don't want to hurt you," he said.

Daniel crept into the kitchen before checking other rooms and was met by Enzo holding Emily with the knife to her throat. Daniel stopped. Enzo spoke, "I won't hurt her, just drop the gun on the floor and push it over with your foot."

Daniel said, "Okay, look, I am doing as you say, now release Emily."

Enzo smiled and said, "Emily, not agent Miles, well Emily you and I are going for a ride and hopefully if you behave you won't get hurt. Although

I can't say that about my unhappy friends out in Italy you upset all those years ago. They have their own agenda for you."

He slipped cuffs on her wrists. Daniel moved and Enzo said to him, "Not a good move if you don't want me to damage the goods."

Daniel stood still, feeling helpless. His eyes met Emily's. She looked apprehensive at what was going to happen to her. Enzo threw cuffs at Daniel, telling him to put them over one wrist and the other through the oven handle. When he had done that, Enzo holding Emily, came over to check they were secure. Then returned to Emily, and got hold of her watch on her wrist and removed it and threw it on the table.

The Enzo said, "I am taking her and don't want anyone trying to follow me, okay, understand?"

Daniel nodded as they left. While Enzo left taking her by the front door exit, he grabbed her coat to cover the cuffs he had put on. He whistled and a van turned up at the front door. The van doors at the back were opened and he pushed her towards it. Inside was a crate. Before she could react someone covered her face and she passed out.

Chapter 6

As soon as he heard the van leave, Daniel pressed his watch to alert the others. Soon someone came to the house and released him from the cuffs. He then updated Charles on the situation. They had planted a device under Emily's skin near her belly button, so they could track her. They did not want to get too close too soon. They knew which airport they were taking her to and had men planted in and around it. Her safety was paramount as she was a willing party to it all and Charles wanted her alive at the end. He owed her that.

Emily, she repeated, that was her name? Yes but her head was in a fog and she was trying to find her way out. A slap on her face, then she blinked. His face, then she saw his eyes. He kissed her cheek, the one he had just slapped.

"You awake now?" I wanted to talk to you before we put you in your padded crate," Enzo said.

"I loved you Emily, you must have felt the same. You kept saying, no, but it was in your eyes. You sold me out. You hurt me, my heart. I cannot let that go. You sent me to jail to rot, you thought. But I got out early, surprise! I sort you out, now I will make you suffer slowly like me," Enzo said in a threatening manner.

She did not know what to say. Yes she had fallen for him but her job would not allow her to take things further. She had to push her emotions to one side. Her job came first before love or happiness, even more so when it was a villain. She could not allow herself to drop her guard. Maybe she had during the assignment. She swallowed hard before replying to him.

"Enzo you know I had to do my job. I could do no more even if I found you pulling me under your spell. It had to stop and I needed to do my job as an agent and capture the gang including you. But surely if you escaped jail early you would want freedom, not this," Emily stated.

He looked longingly into her eyes and said, "I'm Italian, we have passion for love and romance but you English are cold. No this is my only way, however it ends."

He taped her mouth and legs, and changed the handcuffs to tape and then bundled her into the crate saying, "Goodbye my love, see you in Italy when we meet again."

He shut the crate and sealed it up making sure vents were opened, after he had pushed gas into the crate for her to sleep through the journey. He spoke to his men in Italian. They had come over to help along with the men he had hired in the UK who were part of a gang he had got to know. They all knew what they had to do. Flight plans and export papers were all done and ready for them to fly out with Emily in the crate as cargo.

They pulled up outside the gates of the airport, scanning around, all seemed okay, with Enzo directing the van to go over to the plane waiting for them. Paperwork was stamped by the corrupt official who accepted payment for it. They pulled up beside the plane and opened the cargo hold and loaded the crate. The paperwork was all in order, they were ready to go.

That is when the firing started. Hidden among the buildings and vehicles on the tarmac, Charles's men were waiting. The shots were aimed at the men around the van. Bullets fired, hitting the van's tyres, so there was no escape for the men. Then he saw Enzo heading for the plane, and he was trying to aim for his legs. Charles was also trying not to hit the plane due to it being full of fuel and Emily being on board. He had to be careful with his aim.

Charles missed and allowed Enzo to get on board the plane while the gun battle with his men continued. Then Enzo instructed the pilot to start the engines and not to wait for his men. He nodded and started the engines ready for taxying down the runway. Enzo pulled the door shut and sat down where Emily's crate was strapped in. He said, "Don't worry we will soon be away and then you will be mine forever!"

Emily heard him as she came round and had a feeling in the pit of her stomach, thinking that he was going to make her suffer. She had to keep positive and hope that Charles, as promised, would come and get her unless she got a chance to kill Enzo herself. Well she was expecting Charles to rescue her before she got on the plane but sometimes plans don't go as they should.

Enzo gently touched the crate and said, "Our time together will be my pleasure."

Cold shivers ran down her spine as she felt those dark eyes bore through the crate to her. She closed her eyes and prayed Charles would rescue her before Enzo found the tracer planted inside her.

The plane engines roared as it took off while on the ground Charles's men moved in as he knew it was too late to stop the plane but at least he could maybe capture some of the men working with Enzo. Charles approached one of his men with a telephone, which was handed to him, "So you have the tracer and you are following her, good keep me informed when he lands. You need to follow him and report back, thanks," Charles ended the call.

He would have to be patient for news once the plane had landed, then he would send in his elite team to rescue her. He had not wanted it to be like this. His priority was to get her out alive.

The plane was coming in to land at a small airport near Rome, Ciampino which Enzo used a lot and had vehicles waiting for him, plus Mafia men who now worked for him. Since coming out of jail he had formed his own gang. Guys who previously had worked for him had come and joined him again. During his stay in jail he had made many contacts which were very helpful to his line of business, drugs and money laundering and anything else that came his way.

Emily felt the plane land. She was panicking now. She managed to take the tape off her mouth but kept her mouth shut. Then she remembered her small knife strapped to her leg. If she could get to it she could cut through her taped hands and feet. Then when they opened the crate she would surprise them, perhaps? That depended upon how many men were around at the time but she had to try. Her training, she remembered it all. Once an agent always an agent.

Once she felt the plane stop, she held her breath. What next? Enzo waited until the van had backed up to the plane door. Then he opened it and his men took the crate out and put it in the waiting van, while Enzo walked down the steps. A custom officer came over to Enzo and one of his men handed him the documents, which he scanned, and then said something in Italian and they all laughed. A handshake and then an envelope passed to the custom officer, payment from Enzo for his help.

They got into the van and drove away, heading for a place called Calcata, a village standing over a cliff made of volcanic rock, surrounded by green forest. It was neglected in the 60's and so Enzo saw his chance and bought several of the houses away from neighbouring properties. He spent time and money over the years on them, it was his escape and it also had a good cellar for wine and anything else that needed locking away. There he would torture her very slowly, to her last breath.

Another small plane landed soon after Enzo's plane, which taxied and parked. Then an agent walked off the plane thanking the pilot. Speaking in Italian to the authority, he was directed to the building, where inside waited an old friend. Sometimes you have to work with people you hate. The Mafia had a certain hold on different areas but when one of theirs goes off the rails they were prepared to help a little.

Agent Frank had dealings with the Mafia over the years, spoke fluent Italian and was respected by them and vice versa. Agent Frank opened the case with the tracking device and was advised that Enzo had a place out in Calcata and that was the direction, according to the tracking device where he was heading. He was handed keys to a vehicle which was parked out to the front of the airport. Frank thanked him, took the keys and headed out of the airport.

Agent Frank rang Charles. He was told that an elite team of four was coming out via Rome airport and that he needed to liaise with them once he had confirmed she was there. Frank agreed and finished the call. He set off in the car in the direction the tracking device was indicating. He hoped Emily was holding up.

Enzo drove through the village planning what he was going to do to his prize. At the same time Emily had managed with great effect and flexibility, which she did not realise she still had, to find her knife and cut both feet and hands free. She needed a plan as she heard the vans gears grinding as they drove up the steep hills or that is what it felt like. She had no idea where he was taking her but she knew she had to take her chance to escape the crate and whatever lay ahead of her, which would not be a picnic.

The van turned, sliding the crate to one side of the van. Then it stopped, turned and she felt it was going backwards, it stopped and the engine turned off. Enzo instructed the men in Italian, of which Emily caught a couple of words but they did not make sense. She told herself, must practice languages. Then the crate was lifted with her still inside which she thought was strange. It was tilted at an angle which made her slide to the bottom and then it was straightened and rested onto something, a table maybe or floor?

All she could hear now was her slow controlled breathing, waiting for the bottom of the crate to be opened, ready to kick with all her might. The click of the latches came. She kicked as hard as she could, and Enzo was caught off guard and fell backwards, nearly losing his balance. She pushed herself out with the knife in her hand, looking around seeing Enzo half crouched on the floor. They both were still for a second, waiting for the other to make a move. He spoke in calm low tones, "I will not fight you, put the knife down and we can talk. I will not call my men unless you want a fight," he said.

She thought for a while. If he called his men she didn't have a chance. She might be able to wound him but she was not sure whether he was carrying a gun and so he could shoot her before she had a chance with the knife. Weighing up the odds, they were against her.

She surrendered her knife to him. He came over to her and gently took it saying, "Good choice." He drew his gun and aimed at her, then said, "Over there I have a bed for you but I have to chain you as well, in case you decided to escape. I will keep you alive as long as I can but cannot promise my men will. They have a grudge against you like I have and would sooner make it easier to kill you now, rather than prolong your life. We shall see who wins."

He clipped a leg cuff around her ankle with a long chain so she could walk around her bed. There was a bucket in the corner and a jug and bowl to wash. A bottle of water stood on the table beside the bed. Once he had secured her he turned to go and said, "I will see you maybe later, we shall see." He shut the door behind him, then keys turned and bolts slid across.

She looked around her prison; no windows or vents, so her only escape was the door. She was screwed. She needed Charles to break her out. Why had not Enzo checked her body for a tracker or did he know already and wanted them to come for her. Then his gang could have their vengeance. All she knew was that she had a long wait ahead of her and an unknown.

What she did not know was Enzo had cameras watching her in her prison. No doubt that would be the case, so he could watch her as and when he wanted while the rest of the time his men kept an eye on her. Enzo planned to torture her slowly bit by bit to see how long she would last until she begged him for mercy. She sat down on the bed and reached for the water and drank some. When she heard the door being opened, his men came down the steps into the room and removed the crate she had come in. They did not acknowledge her in any way, but as they lifted it off the stainless steel table she saw it was no ordinary one. The table had straps and she knew what that meant but tried to dismiss it from her mind. She would have to wait for her fate.

Chapter 7

She woke with a headache, and felt dehydrated and hungry. She did not know what time it was with no sunlight, or whether it was day or night. It was her natural body clock she would go by. She must have slept, although fitful, as she was exhausted. She looked round the room and noticed another bottle of water had appeared. She drank, but slowly to keep the rest as it looked like they were giving her one a day. No food to weaken her. As she was thinking this she heard the bolts and key in the door. She caught her breath. Enzo appeared with a tray of utensils that looked like a surgeon would use, followed by two men.

They approached her. She backed off as far as the chain would allow her. He spoke. "We can do this the easy way or the hard way. It's up to you."

She moved forward. One of the men took her hands while the other unlocked her leg cuff. They pulled her over to the table and both lifted her on to it, strapping her legs and then her hands to her side. She felt vulnerable. Enzo picked up a scalpel and ripped her top up the front exposing her stomach. She squirmed as she knew what he was about to do. He pulled at her trousers, exposing her belly button.

Enzo said, "What have we here," touching the area where she had had the device inserted. She kept her body still now as she felt the scalpel over her skin. Then a hand appeared over her face and before she could do anything she was unconscious.

She woke in excruciating pain that she had not experienced for a very long time and screamed to help release the pain she was feeling. She tried to lift her head but was still groggy. Then Enzo held above her face the bloody tracker for her to see.

He said, "Sorry I made a bit of a mess trying to get it out."

She asked, "Why leave it so long before you took it out?"

Enzo replied, "I needed them to follow you so I can set a trap for them, then we can have a party." Laughing, he threw the tracker, smashing it on the floor while someone was doing something to her body. They must have numbed the area as she was feeling less and less pain now. Then a dressing was put over it. She was released and told to get off the table and lie down on the bed. The leg cuff was put back on, and they all left her on the bed.

She started to feel where they had stitched her. It was sore but not as bad as it was when she first came round. It was only under the skin but it was still sore. She tried to distract herself and needed to escape, as now she had a weak spot on her body he would use that to torture her.

She woke with a jump. She must have slept. She took a mouthful of water. As she did her stomach reminded her, what they had done to her. Not knowing what time it was she looked around the room. The table was still in its bloody state with the equipment still out but her leg chain was too short for her to reach any of the instruments. Then she looked around the floor to see if she could see any wire, nail or anything to pick the lock of her leg cuff. After a few minutes she spotted something that might work. She turned over on her side to get off the bed and drop down onto a knee. It still hurt but she went down onto the floor and picked up a thin tack pin and hid it in her hand, under her ring. She rose and sat on the

103

bed and took a drink of water. Sitting on the bed, she carefully bent forward to her ankle and rubbed the area where the cuff was. While she did that, she slipped the pin down to her fingers and attempted to pick the lock on the leg cuff at her ankle. She thought to herself, this looks easy in the movies, surely she could do it, half smiling to herself. It was going! She was massaging her ankle in a way not to attract attention. Then she heard a click.

She carefully put the pin back under her ring and lifted her head. She was going to try and lie on the bed without disturbing the leg cuff. She dropped the pin down the side of the bed.

A man walked in. She heard him and turned her head. He had a glass of something and what looked like a cake. He put it down on the table and said, "Eat, he does not want you fading away too quickly." He turned and left shutting the door behind him, bolting and turning the key.

She turned slowly, sat up and looked at what had been left for her. She was hungry. She wondered if the food was drugged. She didn't care, she picked it up and took a bite, it was like necter, sweet and sticky. In the glass, she smelt it. It was milk in a coloured glass. Savouring them both, she ate and drank slowly.

While she was doing that she looked around the room and spotted the hidden camera, yes he was watching her. She needed to plan an escape even though she felt she would not make it. It would be better than being tortured!

She finished the cake and milk, bent down to her ankle and rubbed it, checking it was free, but making sure the cuff stayed shut and secure. She got up and moved backwards and forwards stretching herself seeing how much pain she was in where they had cut her. She was strong. She moved up and down, stretching the leg chain until the moment when she would make her move. She had also noticed some gardening tools in the corner of the room and above the camera. She needed to do this quickly and hoped they were not monitoring her all the time. She had to take her chance.

It took place in slow motion for her. She walked, stretching the chain, pulled free, ran to the tools, then smashed the camera lens with the spade and stopped, spade still in her hand. Her heart was racing waiting for the men or Enzo to come in, spade ready as her weapon. Nothing. She walked over and snatched several instruments from the tray. She carefully walked to the door to see if she could pick the lock, then she heard footsteps running towards the door. She pulled back ready to strike whatever came through the door.

Then voices, shouting, gunfire and then more gunfire near the door, then it flung open. She swung the spade. It stopped above her head, as she realised she was being rescued. She saw familiar faces, two of them, which came through the door towards her. They saw her bloody top and looked at her with concern.

Then she said, "It took you long enough to rescue me, what was the hold up?"

Frank spoke, "Had to get permission for the cavalry but I am sorry, we had to kill Enzo, he gave us no choice."

She took a sudden breath in, a sadness came over her. She knew in her heart of heart that she loved him but because of work she could not show any weakness. The job always came first, but even so, sad that he decided to die rather than go to jail again. She came round and replied, "He did not enjoy being locked up and wanted the freedom. He wanted to pay me back for not loving him and taking that freedom from him. He could not have seen himself going back to jail again."

Frank nodded and gently ushered her out of the cellar. She passed other members of the team and extra men Charles had decided to send at the last minute. There was an ambulance waiting for her to go into to be checked. She was taken straight to it and put inside, while Frank instructed someone to go with her. He shut the doors and banged on the side of the vehicle to send it on its way to the hospital.

Then he turned and instructed the men to clear up the bodies and with the Italian police who were now on the scene with them as well, they worked together.

Chapter 8

Emily felt comfortable now, after surgery. They had checked no damage had been done internally and the wound was sealed properly along with pain killers which had been administered.

They now brought her food and drink but she had also been put on a drip as she was dehydrated. She was sore but she was a good healer. Given time she would soon be back on her feet. After she had eaten, she settled down and slept.

The next thing she knew was Charles gently tapping her shoulder. She opened her eyes. She must have slept long as it was dark outside. He looked at her with concern and said, "How you doing Emily? I am so sorry this has happened to you, we should have arrested Enzo sooner, then perhaps this may not have happened."

Emily said, "You did not know what he was going to do and why. At least you sent the cavalry in for me. Thanks for that."

He laughed, "You're welcome. When the doctors give us the okay with you we will fly you home. You are to stay in hospital as long as you need to, that is an order."

She tried to laugh but it hurt. He kissed her forehead and whispered, "We miss you on the team." Then touching her hand, Charles left her. She shut her eyes again and thought of nice thoughts to dream, beautiful meadows and lakes with mountains covered in snow. Soon she drifted to sleep.

Charles kept his word. She was flown home a few days later and taken to a private hospital where she recuperated for some two weeks.

When she was ready and felt fit enough to go home the doctors let Charles know. She was packing her bags, her back to him, when he walked into her room.

"Well, you ready to go back to retirement after all this excitement? " Charles said.

She turned round, smiling at him and said, "You know with the head problems, I can't come back to be part of the team and I hate desk jobs. So yes, I will go back to my house and enjoy the peace and quiet. I will probably be painting again soon as well. But I will be destroying one very important picture of Enzo in the Piazza Navona, as that part of my life is over." She sighed.

Charles picked up her bag and they both walked out of the hospital into the most wonderful day of blue skies and sun.

Emily thought, it is a good day to be alive!

Lightning Source UK Ltd.
Milton Keynes UK
UKOW04f0124261117
313354UK00001B/15/P